BRUISED

BOOK ONE

TT KOVE

ARCTIC CIRCLE PRESS

CHAPTER 1

"*S*ee you tomorrow, Kaz!" Adam lifted a hand in a wave and hurried down the sidewalk towards the tube station before the rain drenched him through.

I watched him go and only when he was out of sight did I sag back against the brick wall behind me, the tears I'd held back all night overflowing. They streamed down my cheeks, mixing with the rain, and I bent over as my body shook with the force of the sobs I tried my best to keep inside.

Eyes closed, teeth clenched, arms wrapped around my middle… it was all I could do to keep myself in check, but it didn't work. The tears kept coming and my body continued to shake.

A door closing made me freeze—all of me but the tears, anyway, they kept on coming. A pair of black boots entered my line of sight and I slowly lifted my head to stared up at whoever had remained behind after us. I'd thought Adam and I had been the last ones leaving the club after we finished cleaning.

It wasn't a colleague. It was my boss.

"Kasey?" He eyed me carefully.

I bowed my head quickly, horrified at being caught crying my heart out by my boss. My very scary boss who everyone tip-toed around. "I'm s-so-sorry," I managed to get out, but I couldn't for the life of me stop crying. My chest and stomach hurt and it only made it worse, because I couldn't stop and the pain only added to all the shit.

"What's wrong?" He was at my side now, looming over me to the point he blocked out most of the rain.

"I d-didn't g-ge-get in!" That's what hurt most of all. I'd dreamt of going to the London Contemporary Dance School for *years* and now I'd had my chance, I'd *failed*. I had to apply again, wait a year for auditions, and then another year again to start at the school if I did get in.

"School, huh?" he scoffed, and for a second I thought he'd walk past and leave me there—but then his hands cupped around my face, bringing my head up so he could look at me. "It's not the end of the world, surely?"

It *was*. I was supposed to go to school, make something of myself, but like I failed everything else, I'd also failed this. "Auditions a-are a y-year in a-ad-advance." Two years at the most… and what if I failed to get in next year too? That would be yet more years where I wouldn't be making something of myself.

What would I do? Keep working at the club? A job I was shit at because I was clumsy and always dropped glasses or bottles. I couldn't do anything right. Dance was the one thing I was good at—but clearly I wasn't good enough.

He sighed, thumbs gently brushing under my eyes.

It was… nice. No one ever did that for me. Kian hugged me if I cried in front of him, and Silver could do that too… but if I cried in front of Alistair all he'd do was backhand me and tell me to grow up and be a man. I couldn't go home to him like this, it wouldn't end well. He had no patience.

"Hey, come on." One hand slipped from my face and gripped my shoulder instead. He steered me away from the club. "Where do you live?"

"I can't go home," I whispered, reaching up to wipe furiously at my eyes.

"Why not?" he asked, frowning down at me.

"I just c-can't. Not like th-this." The damn tears

wouldn't stop. And neither would the rain. It was fitting for my mood, but it didn't make it any better.

"Well, you're drenched, I can't just leave you out here to freeze." He squeezed my shoulders and it felt... safe. "Come with me. I live just around the corner."

I swallowed heavily. *Go with him? To his* home? But... I shut off the various scenarios playing through my head, the result of too many horror flicks. He was my boss, he wouldn't hurt me. He actually seemed worried about me, even if I always made a mess. I wasn't a good bartender; hell, I wasn't even half decent.

He whipped out a key to unlock a door, led us into a hall, and then up the stairs. We both trekked water after us, both drenched, but I still couldn't stop crying, so the cold was the last of my worries.

It seemed he lived on the top floor. I hardly got a look inside his flat when he led me in there, because he didn't bother turning on the lights as he shoved me into the bathroom.

I blinked as he turned *those* lights on, trying to get used to the brightness with my sore eyes, but then he threw a towel over my head, effectively blocking all light out.

"Sit." He pushed me down onto something, likely the toilet seat, and proceeded to gently rub the towel over my hair. I'd styled it nicely before work last night, but it must be a right mess now. "Do you want a shower?"

A hot shower... That would be nice. "There wouldn't be any point. My clothes are still wet."

"You can borrow some of mine." He dropped the towel over my shoulders, rubbing it gently over my neck before he unzipped my jacket. I just sat there, gazing at him in wonder as he took it off me in one swift motion.

Borrow his clothes... He was way bigger than me. Taller, wider, more muscular. I was a runt compared to him. He'd got rid of his own jacket some place and now sat in front of me wearing only a tee. His biceps flexed and he had a full-sleeve tattoo on that arm that flexed with his muscles. I couldn't study it in detail, but what I did see was something resembling an eye, a clock, trees maybe? Then he straightened back up and turned to get a bigger towel from under the sink.

"You get in the shower. I'll find some clothes for you." With that, he left me alone in the bathroom, the door clicking shut softly after him.

I drew in a shaky breath as I stared at the closed door. At work, everyone seemed almost afraid of Wynn —said he didn't tolerate any bullshit, that he easily fired people. Why he hadn't fired me was a mystery, considering how much I messed up, but... He was kind. He hadn't had to take me home. He didn't have to lend me his clothes or his shower or anything. But he did.

I undressed slowly, hands shaking a little. Some tears still trickled, but the earlier torrent had stopped. I fumbled with the shower for a bit until I got the temperature of the water just right, then I stepped in and pulled the wide glass door closed.

My eyes closed as I tilted my head up to meet the spray of hot water. It felt nice against my cold skin and it soothed the sadness just a tiny bit. It didn't disappear, not by a long shot—it never did nowadays—but it sure helped.

I didn't dare stay in the shower too long, though, in case I outstayed my welcome. I stepped out dripping wet, grabbed the big, fluffy towel he'd discarded on the counter, and wrapped it around me.

Shit, clothes. He hadn't come into the bathroom before I undressed, and he clearly hadn't been in while I'd been in the shower either. I shuffled over to the door, cracked it open to see if he was nearby... then spotted the promised clothes on the floor right in front of me.

A shaky breath left me and I scooped them up, quietly shutting the door after me. *Why is he so kind to me?* There was a T-shirt, joggers, and boxers. All too big on me, but they were better than slipping on my wet clothes. I looked like a little kid drowning in grown-up clothes, but it would have to do.

I hung up the towels, the one he'd used on my hair earlier and the big, fluffy one, then gathered my clothes in my arms and stepped out of the safety of the bathroom to face him.

He was in the open-plan kitchen, pouring himself a glass of Coke. He glanced up, dark eyes locking on me. "You want some?"

"Yes, please." I licked my lips nervously. "What about my clothes?"

He poured Coke into the second glass—clearly meant for me—and slid it over the counter. "Here you go. I'll take those." He came around, took the clothes from me, and went to stuff them in the washer. "I'll put them on a short programme, then put them in the drier once it's done."

I blinked. Washer and drier, that took time. And it was already late.

He glanced at me over his shoulder. "Unless you want to take them home with you?"

I shook my head quickly. I still couldn't go home. I couldn't face Alistair like this. Most days I didn't want to face him at all, but he was my flatmate so I didn't have a choice.

A crooked grin appeared on his face. "Don't worry. I don't expect anything in return."

My eyes widened in surprise. *Did he think I thought...?* Then again, if he had expected anything... I wouldn't be entirely opposed to it. He was handsome, kind... kinder than my own boyfriend. Not that Alistair was my boyfriend, he was quite vehement about us being a couple—at least outside our flat. He wasn't much of a boyfriend inside it either, where he changed between talking down to me and slapping me around.

I took the glass and emptied half of it in one swallow, thirsty after crying so much earlier. My throat hurt too, for the same reason. The Coke helped a little.

"So what's got you down?" He was around the counter again now, leaning against it, glass in one hand as he gazed at me. "You've been down all night."

I blinked. Blushed. "You've been watching me?" Probably to see how many mistakes I made. How many glasses I managed to break or how many orders I could mix up.

"Yeah." He didn't even deny it.

"I'm sorry." I bowed my head. "I know I shouldn't bring my problems to work—"

"True. No one should do that. Yet everyone does anyway. It's the way it is." He shrugged, sounding like it didn't matter to him. Maybe it didn't.

"I had my audition today. I applied last year and the auditions are now for enrolment next September, and... I messed up." The glass clinked softly as I put it down on the counter. I wrapped both hands around it, squeezing. "So I didn't get in. Now I have to wait till next year and hope I get in the year after that again. It's just… so many years."

"Does it have to be the London Contemporary Dance School?"

He remembered. "Yeah. I want a degree in Contemporary Dance. I'm much better at that than I am ballet, so… yeah, I like it better. And I don't want to move, because my family's here." I would like to move away from Alistair, but I couldn't afford to live on my own. "The plan was to get in, work for the next year so I could save up some money until school started. But now…" Now I didn't know what to do.

"Well, you've still got a job," he drawled. "Now you can just save up even more."

How much longer would I have the job though? I was shit at it. I'd only got it because Adam had vouched for me. I didn't dare say that out loud to my boss though. That was a sure way to dig my grave. Not to mention he probably knew, if he was usually out and about in the club itself.

I couldn't afford to lose the job. I couldn't become dependent on Alistair. He'd probably love it, but I was trying my best to eventually get away from him. Maybe I would have to bite the bullet and slink back to my brother, but… my pride wouldn't let me. Kian hadn't liked that I moved out to be with my boyfriend —he and his lover were the only ones who knew about my relationship with Alistair. They liked him, because they didn't know the truth, but they hadn't liked me moving in with him.

"There you go, looking sad again."

My head shot up.

"And there are those wide, startled eyes." He narrowed *his* eyes at me.

Sad again? *Wide, startled eyes…* Had he watched me all night? Or… wasn't tonight the first night he'd watched me?

He leaned forward a little. "Besides your botched audition today, are you all right?"

I nodded quickly. "I'm fine." *Just peachy*.

His eyes narrowed again. "You sure about that? Because to me you usually look like a bundle of high-strung nerves."

I swallowed audibly.

He discarded his glass and came around the counter to stand in front of me. He tipped my chin up so I had no choice but to gaze up at him. He kept his fingers on my chin, thumb stroking gently.

It made me weak in the knees, as cliché as that sounded. My lips parted ever-so-slightly, breath stuttering the tiniest bit.

He took a step closer, bringing our bodies *almost*

into contact. But then he halted and simply stood there and stared at me.

I licked my lips, nervous and aroused at the same time. His eyes followed my tongue and that's when I knew for sure that this man... this big, butch, tattooed, handsome man who could probably have everyone he wanted... wanted *me*. And if that didn't make my breath stutter in my throat and my heart beat wildly, nothing would.

"Kasey," he murmured, thumb stroking softly over my bottom lip. Then he closed his eyes and turned his head away. "When I said I didn't expect anything in return for helping you out, I meant it." He seemed to steel himself for something, lips pressing tight together, frown deepening. He took a step back, thumb dropping from my lip...

And I stepped forward, right back into his space. "I don't mind," I whispered, because damn, he was the best thing to have happened to me in so long. My life was shit, had been for a long time and even more so after today, and I deserved something good for a change.

He was good. He wasn't forceful with me, didn't talk to me like I was an idiot, didn't make my decisions for me, and best of all... he didn't hurt me.

My cheeks were on fire, but I drew from some unknown place inside me and said, more in a whisper than the confidence I'd tried for, "You can kiss me if you want."

He let out a breath. His lips tilted up on one side, and then... then he bent down and pressed them to mine.

CHAPTER 2

I gasped, body arching up against him. His strong arms wrapped around me, pulling me up close as he slipped his tongue past my lips.

He's got a tongue piercing, was my first thought as my own tongue butted against the steel knob, then I ceased thinking at all as pleasure and instinct took over.

He picked me up like I weighed nothing and carried me into his bedroom. There he gently put me down in the middle of his huge bed, all while he kept kissing me. His hands, which had grabbed my arse as he lifted me, now moved up under the baggy T-shirt to encounter my flushed, naked skin.

His mouth left mine to attach to my neck instead and I tilted my head back on a low moan. Very low, as making noise during sex was a big no-no. Or so I'd been told, anyway.

"This okay?" Wynn asked, thumb brushing over my nipple.

"Mmm." This was more than okay.

"Good." And with that, he easily slipped the T-shirt off me, then sat up slightly to pull his own off as well.

He was... magnificent, there was no other word for it. Tanned, tattooed, *ripped*. He wasn't just toned, he had actual washboard abs. As well as a dark smattering of hair over his chest and down to his trousers.

I was nothing compared to him. I was slim and toned yes because of all the dancing I did, and my skin wasn't exactly pale—thanks to my mum's Asian genes —but I didn't work out regularly like he obviously did. I wasn't tall or broad or fit. I was a small, slim, femme guy... and if Wynn wanted to, he could crush me.

"Don't be embarrassed." He grabbed my wrists and moved my arms up over my head, holding them there with one hand while the other splayed over my chest. "You're gorgeous."

Now that was a first, but I went with it. I didn't believe him, but he clearly wanted to shag me, so he was probably laying it on a bit thick just to get me there. He didn't have to though, I was already *here*. I wanted this just as much as he did.

His mouth, again attached to my neck, moved

downwards. Sucking, licking, kissing his way down over my collarbone, my nipple, and down my stomach until he reached the hem of the joggers. He hesitated only briefly—perhaps to see if I had anything to say about it—and then he let go of my hands to pull both the joggers and boxers down and off.

Cold air licked over my naked skin… until he was back over me, covering me completely as he dove into another deep kiss. I clutched at his upper arms, feeling the muscles flex under his skin.

His hand circled my cock and I arched my hips into it, wanting, begging for more. More touch, more heat, more pressure. I should do the same for him too, I figured, so I hooked my fingers under the hem of his trousers.

"No." He batted my hands away.

"But—You—" I stared at him as he moved down my body again, lips ghosting over my stomach before his chin butted against the head of my dick. "I should—"

He met my gaze. "Don't guys go down on you?" His lips were *so close* to my dick.

"Not… really." Alistair never deigned to go down on me. He probably thought doing that would make him gay. As if fucking my arse didn't make him that to begin with. *But don't think about him!* He didn't belong here, not with this fine specimen of a man.

He grinned wryly. "Then lie down and *enjoy*."

It felt wrong to be on the receiving end of a blow job. To enjoy all on my own without doing anything in return. I was usually the one who did the cock-sucking—and who then turned around to spread my arse so they'd have a hole to fuck with all their might. That's the kind of sex I was used to, not this... this slow, torturous pleasure he was currently dishing out.

He stroked me and his lips briefly sucked my head in, but then let it pop back out. He pulled the foreskin down before he licked all the way up my shaft... and then finally took me into his heat, tongue pressing against the underside while he sucked.

My hands fisted in the sheets and I strangled my moans before they could be voiced as much as I was able to. I swear my toes curled, that's how good he was at this. The tongue piercing... that was also something else and he knew exactly how to use it to give me the most pleasure.

I clamped a hand over my mouth as I came, muffling the voice I could no longer keep inside. My stomach hollowed, showing off my ribs, but it didn't matter because he wasn't even looking. He was still sucking, swallowing every single last drop coming out of me.

When I was empty, I lay boneless, staring up at the

ceiling without really seeing it, enjoying the post-orgasmic bliss.

I didn't notice he'd moved until he pushed my legs further apart and scooted in-between them. *Here it comes*, I thought, trying to stay relaxed as I waited for his cock to breach me... but it didn't.

He was still on his knees, trousers and underwear off, and he wanked himself off over me. His dick was flushed, straining, and... he had several piercings on the underside of it. I'd heard about them, but couldn't remember what they were called. Something ladder, if I wasn't mistaken. And he had a Prince Albert, but not a ring that was usual in porn. It was a bar like the others, except a little more curved.

I'd never seen genital piercings in real life before. It was hot. And I wondered what it would be like if he fucked me. Would it feel any different than an un-pierced cock? Surely I'd feel them? And what was it like for him? A lot more sensitive, I'd reckon.

"Like it?" he asked, grinning wryly. That seemed to be his standard grin, really, like he could only move the one side of his face while the other stayed in a neutral expression.

"Y-yeah." What would it be like to suck a dick with all those piercings?

His hand moved quickly, expertly getting himself off. His eyes closed briefly as he shot his first load, to land on my lower stomach, some of it tangling in my short, trimmed pubes. His neck strained as he tilted his head back, stroking himself faster, squeezing harder, until he had nothing more to give either.

"Fuck." He collapsed at my side, so close our shoulders and arms pressed together.

"I thought you'd want to fuck me," I blurted out, swirling my index finger through his come on my stomach.

He chuckled. "It's too late for that. Or too early, depending on how you look at it." He grabbed my hand, brought it to his lips, and licked the semen off my fingers. Then he met my gaze straight on. "When I fuck you, I want to take my time."

My face flushed red, but I couldn't look away. His eyes were dark, but they held a promise. A promise of great sex to come, and just… *yes*. I was so down for that. I smiled through my embarrassment, secretly pleased that he clearly had plans for more, not just this one time.

"Go to sleep, Kasey." He curled around me, wrapping one strong arm around my waist. "Everything will be better tomorrow."

I let myself be moved onto my side so he could be the big spoon to my little one, and I put my hand over his. But his words… those I didn't believe. In the morning I would have to face my life again and that wasn't something I looked forward to. If we could've just stayed in bed like this forever, I thought I'd be happy, but that wasn't possible. I had to wake up, had to leave, had to go home, where Alistair lived and ruled.

But for now I wasn't going to think about *him*. I was going to enjoy the one good thing that *had* happened to me today—in months, really. Wynn was a warm, calming, heavy presence against my back. After the day I'd had, I didn't need much else to fall right asleep. The orgasm I'd just had probably helped too.

I WOKE UP ALONE.

For a brief moment I was disoriented, looking around in wonder as I realised I wasn't in my own bedroom. The sheets were rumpled, but the space next to me was cold, so Wynn was long gone.

A sigh left me and I sat up slowly to look for my clothes. Or his clothes, as it were. Turned out I didn't have to, because my own clothes were lying neatly folded on the bedside table. When I touched them, they were still warm from the dryer.

The sheets pooled in my lap and I looked down at myself to see how dirty I was after he'd come on me. Turned out I wasn't. There was absolutely no evidence of semen on me at all—and I clearly remembered some of it trickling into my pubes.

He cleaned me up. My face heated. I pulled my clothes on in quick, jerky movements. Was this his way of saying *thanks for a nice night but off you go*? I dreaded leaving the bedroom, to find out what waited me out there. Was he even out there? Well, he had to be, this was his flat, he wouldn't leave me alone in it. Would he?

I couldn't keep sitting on the bed, so I crossed the room and opened the door slowly—and was met by the smell of food.

"Morning," Wynn greeted, back to me as he worked in the kitchen. "I made breakfast."

"Oh." I blinked, completely taken aback.

He glanced over his shoulder. "You've got time to eat right?"

I nodded quickly and sat down at the table as he motioned me to. Minutes later, he sat a plate with a full English down in front of me.

"Water, tea, or juice?"

"Juice, thank you." I didn't know what to say. This was… unexpected.

A glass filled to the brim of orange juice arrived in front of me next, and then he sat down opposite me with a replica of my own breakfast. I tried for a smile, but I was pretty sure it fell short.

"I didn't know what you liked, but I figured a full English is always a safe bet." He raised an eyebrow questioning.

"This is great," I hurried to say because I didn't want to sound ungrateful. "It's just... no one's ever made breakfast for me before." No one had ever done any of the things he'd done. Taken care of me, comforted me, given me pleasure without expecting me to give anything in return. And now this...

His gaze, as dark as ever, told me nothing. His face was expressionless. But he seemed a little tense. I didn't know why, but he'd gone to the trouble of making a proper breakfast for us, so... it couldn't be that he wanted me gone, right?

I hadn't eaten since dinner yesterday, and that hadn't been a particularly satisfying meal as I'd been hurrying between my audition and getting ready for work. "This is really good," I said after I swallowed a bite of eggs and hash-browns.

"I know," he said, not self-conscious in the least. "I know how to cook."

I wasn't all that good at it. Mum liked to cook, but I'd never wanted to learn. And Kian and Silver... they went out for take-away more often than not. It wasn't exactly healthy, but it was quick and easy. "Did someone teach you how to cook?" If I'd let Mum teach me, I could make lots of tasty dishes—even Korean ones, but as it was, I had no clue.

He snorted. "I taught myself. I've been alone for a long time."

What did that mean? He hadn't lived with someone in long? Or that he didn't have *anyone*? Speaking of, I had no idea how old he was. He couldn't be around my age, as he was an acquaintance of my brother, so it was more likely that he was around Kian's age. At least five years older then, but probably more. I didn't dare ask. That would be rude, right?

"Do you only work at the club?" he asked, effectively changing the subject and making sure I didn't blurt out the question of age.

"Yeah." Though now I wasn't facing an audition I'd probably have to find another one to earn more money. So I could finally get away from Al. If my goal couldn't be to earn a degree from the London Contemporary Dance School, then it was damn well going to be get as far away from Alistair as humanly possible.

"You working tonight?" His gaze was steady, not leaving me for a moment.

"Shouldn't you know that?" I countered. "Don't you set up the schedule?" It was his club, after all.

He chuckled. "I've got someone who does that shit for me. As well as hire people. All I do is the paperwork."

"That's hardly *all* you do," I scoffed, not believing him for a second. Owning and running one of London's biggest gay nightclubs couldn't be as easy as doing some simple *paperwork*.

"It basically is." He stretched his arms, hooking them behind his back. "Delegating work makes for a much smoother operation. And less work for me."

I wasn't sure if he was taking the piss or not, so I decided to move the conversation along. "Yeah, I work tonight."

His gaze got all intense again. "Then do you have plans before work?"

"No." What was he getting at? Did he... did he want *us* to do something? My heart started beating faster at that thought, at the hope that this wasn't the end. That it hadn't just been a one-off.

He chuckled. "You don't have to look like a deer caught in headlights. I'm not going to force you to do anything."

"I—I'm not! I mean, I don't think that, I'm not—" Damn it, I couldn't get the words out properly and I scowled unhappily down at what remained of my breakfast. "I'm sorry. I didn't think you would, I was just surprised you want to—" My head shot up as he pushed away from the table.

He grabbed his empty plate, walked past me... and

then reached out to ruffle my hair. "You're sweet, Kasey."

My face flushed again and I stuffed the rest of the sausage in my mouth, chewing instead of giving a stupid answer back, like the childish *am not*.

He was in the kitchen now, rinsing the plate and putting it in the dishwasher. Then he was behind me, hands landing gently on my shoulder, squeezing just the tiniest bit. "Not a fan of beans?"

I stared at the beans I'd moved out of the way from the rest. "No. I'm sorry."

"Nothing to be sorry for." He whisked the plate away, rinsing it, putting it in the dishwasher, exactly like he'd done with his own. Speaking of, he'd cleaned everything he'd used to make breakfast. The counters themselves gleamed.

He's a bit of a neat freak, huh? I filed that information away because I didn't feel comfortable enough to point it out.

"Kasey?" he said then, turning back around to face me as soon as everything was squeaky clean. He crossed his arms, head tilting a little.

"Yeah?" He sounded *serious*. A serious tone like that never boded well for me.

"Spend the day in bed with me?"

I blinked, taken aback.

He blew out a breath and looked away. "It's okay."

Okay? "No—"

"I'm your boss," he spoke almost to himself now, not paying me any mind. "It's not ethically correct to shag your employee. But it's fine. I'm not going to make it awkward for you."

Awkward… God, he seemed so sure of himself but right now he's a right idiot. "I want to," I blurted out, a bit more hotly than intended. I stopped, swallowed, then met his surprised gaze. "Yes, Wynn, I want to spend the day in bed with you."

For the first time since he comforted me outside the club last night, both sides of his lips tilted up in a tiny little smile—but I didn't need to see more of it. He wasn't the kind of person to smile, even I knew that the little I'd seen of him, but right now he *did*. Because of me.

Now that was enough to boost anyone's ego, even mine.

CHAPTER 3

*H*is skin was warm, his body rock hard. There wasn't a single soft spot on him, no fat, just solid muscle. And he was full of ink: both his arms had full-sleeve tattoos, but that wasn't all. He had a chest piece, tattoos on his neck, and over his shoulders, partway down his back.

If I wasn't so damn horny, I might've wanted to study his tattoos more closely, but as it was I was more interested in his dick. It was fully hard, curving upwards, the piercings gleaming in the daylight shining in through the window.

He sat on the bed and I straddled his thighs, fingers brushing almost shyly over his cock, afraid I'd hurt him if I touched him wrong. Then again, he'd wanked himself off quite vigorously last night and that hadn't seemed to hurt.

"Is it okay?" I asked as I wrapped a hand around his thick length.

"Mmm."

"It doesn't hurt?" I didn't dare squeeze too hard.

He chuckled. "No, the piercings make everything *better*. Even so, I don't think you could hurt me even if you *really* tried."

I scowled up at him, but I knew he was right. He was so damn big compared to me, so fit. He could crush me if he wanted. He was a lot more intimidating than Alistair… yet I didn't feel afraid when I was with him at all. If anything, he made me feel safe. He hadn't done anything to hurt me. In fact, he'd gone out of his way to make me feel good.

"I want to suck it," I whispered, gazing back down at his dick. It transfixed me. I had no idea what it would be like with piercings in the mix but I was dying to find out.

"Be my guest." He leant back slightly, bracing his arms on the bed behind him.

I slipped off his lap and he spread his legs, giving me the space I needed in-between them. A clear, translucent bead of pre-come glistened at his slit and I licked it off. *Salty. Mmm.* His cock was a masterpiece waiting to be worshipped and I wanted to put all my skills to use doing just that—and I was good at sucking cock, I'd done nothing else for years until I felt ready to take a dick up my arse.

More pre-come glistened at his slit. I ignored it for now in favour of moving my hand between his cock and stomach, holding it loosely but firmly, and then I ran my tongue up the row of piercings. It was strange —the tips of the piercings were cool, quite different from the hot member they pierced.

He groaned, hips moving slightly like he wanted to buck up into my mouth, but he stayed still. I gave him what he wanted; wrapping my lips around the head, licking up the pre-come, and then slowly sliding down, taking his entire length in. The beaded tip of the Prince Albert piercing nudged the back of my throat, but I'd long since managed to overcome my gag-reflex. I'd had to—rather forcefully.

But this wasn't forceful. Wynn stayed still, arse firmly planted on the bed. He didn't fuck my mouth, didn't grab my hair and force me to take his cock further or suck him faster. No, he didn't touch me at all, just let me do exactly as I pleased. And *that* turned *me* on.

I reached behind my own legs to fist my dick while my other hand held onto his. I sucked him eagerly, loving the feel of the hot, heavy length in my mouth, on my tongue. Loving the taste of his salty pre-come, how it kept leaking, self-lubricating.

"Do you like to be fucked, Kasey?"

I looked up and he sat there, gazing down at me with half-lidded eyes. His breathing was heavy, his stomach muscles taut.

"Because I *really* want to fuck you," he continued, voice low and hoarse and needy. "And if you continue what you're doing, you're gonna make me come."

I let his dick go with a loud *pop*. Saliva and pre-come followed my lips from the tip of his cock, connecting us a little longer.

He brandished a condom packet in front of my eyes. "However you want it. You're in charge."

Why did he keep being so nice to me? He seemed like the type of macho guy who was always in control, yet here he was offering control to tiny little me. I knew what I wanted though—the same thing he did. I rolled the condom on his slick dick, he handed me a tube of lube, and I climbed back up to straddle his lap.

With a good amount of slick spread over my crack and over the condom, I braced my own hands on his shoulders as I rose up. I knew he was looking at me, but I couldn't make myself meet his gaze as I positioned myself. I liked this part, I *did*, but it was still embarrassing to be watched so intently while I was the one doing all the work.

"Ahh," I moaned as he breached me. "Oh, God!" It burned as his cock stretched my hole open. I hadn't had sex in a while and whenever I had sex, it wasn't often it included anal. But taking it slow was the way to go and I did. His piercings stuck out a little from both sides and I felt them as he slid into me too. I didn't stop until my arse rested in his lap though.

I blinked my eyes open, not aware I'd even closed them, and found his face close to mine. His eyes were open, alert, and just as intense as they'd been earlier.

"Feel good?" he asked, but he didn't wait for the answer as he busied my lips with a kiss.

I was full, but it was a good kind of full, and I moved my hips experimentally. *Oh yes, this…* "*Ahhh!*"

"That's it," he murmured, lips sliding feather-light over my own. "Let me hear your voice. Let me hear how much you love my dick in your arse."

Now he'd made me aware of the sounds I'd made, I immediately clammed up. But I didn't stop moving. No, I rose back up, slammed down, up again till only his tip was inside, back down so my arse cheeks slapped against his thighs. My thighs burned, this wasn't a position I was usually in, and I faltered after a little while.

"Want me to take care of you?" His lips brushed my ear now, voice low, seductive.

"Y-yeah," I stuttered, clinging to his shoulders as he

grabbed my arse and quickly flipped us over. This was more what I was used to, being on my back, legs spread, with his weight on me, pushing me into the mattress, cock fucking me ruthlessly. I couldn't even seem to catch my breath properly, the pleasure was so intense.

"How do you like it? Fast?" He kept up the ruthless pace he'd set. "Or slow?" Then slowed down, only rocking against me. *How the hell am I supposed to choose just one?* Both were good in their own way. "Or both?"

"B-both." Definitely both. I couldn't pick just one of them.

"Good." And he quickened the pace again.

I didn't know if I should cling to him or grab the sheets or cover my mouth. The sounds that left me were *loud* and wanton and definitely not me—but no one had ever asked me how I liked it either. No one had ever made sure sex was good for *me*. As long as guys had a hole to stick their dick in, whether a mouth or an arse, they seemed to be happy, for the most part.

Not Wynn. Wynn cared what I thought, what I felt, what gave me pleasure. And in the process he felt pleasure too. His hips snapped back and forth, cock thrusting into me in a fast, hard rhythm. But it wasn't too hard, not too fast. It didn't hurt. It was so good I didn't know what to do with myself.

My legs, which rested over the crook of his arms,

trembled. My toes curled. I grabbed onto his shoulders, holding on for dear life and pretty sure my fingernails dug into his skin, but it didn't matter in that moment because it was so damn good—

And he slowed, rocking us gently, face buried in my neck, strong arms embracing me. I still clung to him, but not with my nails now, instead I wrapped my arms properly around him, one hand sliding up to tangle in his coarse, black hair.

I was still bent almost in half, with my own cock resting, forgotten, against my stomach, leaking pre-come.

"You feel good," he murmured, breath fanning over my skin, giving me tingling goose-bumps. "So tight around my dick, so warm and pliant in my arms—" He did one long thrust with his hips, burying himself inside me, then went back to the slow, rocking rhythm he'd established.

My eyes had closed at some point, and I wasn't in any hurry to open them. The all-consuming desire of the hard and fast fuck of earlier had been replaced by a more content, easy-going sort of desire. The sort where I could fuck like this all night, whereas earlier all I'd wanted was to get off right away—because it was all about chasing the orgasm then, whereas now it was all about prolonging it.

Wynn lifted his head off my neck, then his lips

fastened to mine. Mine were already parted and he wasted no time diving his tongue into my mouth. It was a deep, but lazy kiss, and I sucked on his tongue, lapped my own over his lips, enjoying whatever he gave me.

Until he quickened the speed again, because then it was all about chasing my orgasm. He didn't reach for my cock, however, and I was too busy clinging to him to bring myself off. *Fuck it, maybe I'll come without so much as touching my dick.* That would be something.

"Ahh, fuck!" Wynn wrenched away, sat up on his knees, pulled the condom off and proceeded to stroke his cock, shooting almost immediately. One spurt landed on my stomach, right beneath my navel, the other in my pubes, and the last over my rock-hard flushed dick.

Wynn didn't waste any time—as soon as he was done, he bent down and took *my* cock in his mouth, sucking me into wet heat.

A sound, something between a groan and a sob, left me. I grabbed his head, tangling my fingers in his hair and *tried*—I really did—to not force him to stay down. He seemed to get the message anyway, because he deep-throated me—

And I came with a shout.

He pulled off and stroked me through my orgasm,

milking every single drop from me so it mixed with his own come on my skin.

I dropped my arms over my eyes, completely worn out and flushed and empty and heavy. And a little bit embarrassed because I'd made so much sound, but he didn't seem to mind, so I tried to push that away.

His tongue ran over my skin, lapping up our come.

I let my hands flop to the bed and lifted my head slightly so I could watch. The pink muscle was slick with saliva and semen, and the tongue stud stood out in the middle of it, flexing as he lapped at the come under my navel.

My breathing took it's time calming down, my chest rising and falling quickly. I couldn't take my eyes off the sight of him eating our spunk—and at the same time I wished I could taste too.

I can though. "Wynn?"

"Hmm?" He flicked his gaze up at me.

"Come here." I motioned for him to move up. "I want a taste." Better say it so he didn't swallow.

He grinned, that familiar wry grin, and crushed his lips to mine. His tongue pushed into my mouth, bringing with it the salty, bitter semen. I didn't know if we tasted any different from each other and I didn't care. All that mattered was that it was *our* come and we were sharing it and I'd never thought it would be so hot.

I loved sucking cock and I liked come—I'd gladly swallow if guys wanted to come in my mouth—but this... this was something else. In my experience, guys weren't that keen on tasting their own come. Or mine. Yet here we were, sharing ours.

Our lips parted slowly, hesitantly. He caressed my face as he pulled away, nose rubbing against mine. "Who knew you were so dirty in bed, huh?" he murmured.

"Huh?"

He chuckled, deep in his throat. "Like I said, you always seem like a bundle of exposed nerves. When people talk to you, you tend to look like a deer caught in headlights." He dragged his lips over my chin. "But now, during sex... damn."

I stared up at him, not quite understanding. "You... you've been watching me?" It hadn't just been last night? It wasn't often I saw Wynn around the club when I was at work—so where could he have gleaned any sort of information on me from?

"Yeah, I've been watching you." He met my gaze and held it, completely unapologetic. Then he dropped the bombshell, "I've been watching you ever since you started working at the club."

CHAPTER 4

"*I've been watching you ever since you started working at the club.*" That's what he'd just said. And that was… two months ago. I could only remember noticing him a handful of times in that time.

"Does that freak you out?" He rolled off me and sat up, dragging a hand through his messy hair. He seemed almost… resigned to the fact.

"No," I said quickly because it *didn't*. It didn't freak me out at all. Maybe it should, but… Wynn hadn't done anything. He'd watched me, yeah, but he hadn't tried to talk to me or sleep with me in all that time.

Back in college, when I'd majorly fancied Alistair, and he'd been in his last year with me in the year below… He'd noticed how I felt and he'd exploited it. And I'd been happy to be exploited because he liked me back. Except he hadn't really. He'd liked getting his rocks off—having me suck him off wherever we could sneak off to. And it was always sneaking around. I'd been sworn to secrecy.

Still, I'd done it. Because he'd only used me for sex back then and I'd mistaken it for more—the slapping and beatings hadn't started until I moved in with him. As flatmates—and only my brother and his boyfriend knew the real reason. Still, they didn't know the truth, not the whole truth. They *liked* Al, thought he was a great guy. And I couldn't tell them what he was really like, because Al would kill me. And would they even believe me?

"Hey…" Wynn's hand caressed my cheek. "You sure you're not freaking out? You look like you are. I swear, I wasn't going to approach you at all, but you kind of threw that out the window when you stood outside my club crying like that. I couldn't *not* help you out."

I swallowed. "Why weren't you—?" He wasn't going to approach me? At all? Why not? *Maybe he's more the suffer in silence type of guy.* He seemed like it anyway.

He retracted his hand and I felt the loss of its warmth and heaviness. I wanted it back. "Because, Kasey, like I said, you seem like a bundle of nerves. And I'm not a nice person."

Now that was the biggest sack of shit I'd ever heard. "Where'd you get that from? You've been nothing but kind to me." I felt exposed, lying on my back naked like this, flaccid dick sticky with spit and come. But he was the same, so, if he didn't try to cover up I wasn't going to either.

That wry grin was back in place. "That's because I like you."

"Then what—" What was he getting at? If he was nice to me because he liked me, what was all this about not being a nice person? He *was* nice and he'd just admitted it, yet his previous admittance didn't make any sense.

"I'm sure you've noticed that people don't tend to like me very much," he said drily. "I'm sure if your brother knew you were with me right now, he would not be happy."

So he was aware I was Kian's little brother. "My brother doesn't run my life for me. He can't decide who I want to be with or not." He would rather see me with Al instead of Wynn, that I was sure of, but they all had it backwards… Alistair was the one who wasn't a nice person—he just seemed like that from the outside, whereas Wynn was the one who'd put my needs first ever since he caught me crying last night. Al would've never done what Wynn had done, not for me anyway. Probably for his friends—except the sex part, though even that I couldn't be sure of—but to his friends he *was* a nice guy.

"Hey." He stared at me again. "I don't like that expression on you."

I jerked back a little. "What expression?" There was much Al didn't like about me, my tendency to be extremely emotional first on the list.

He frowned, reaching out to smooth his thumb over my forehead. "Like you're thinking about something bad, something you'd rather have been without."

Oh. Well, he was right. I'd rather have been without Al at all if I'd known how it would end up. But I'd been a gullible fool back at college, taken whatever scraps of his affection I could get when it hadn't really been any affection at all. He'd just been in it for a hot mouth to suck his dick. Not once had he sucked mine—or ever really touched it much, come to think of it.

Yet, Wynn… the first thing he'd done was suck me off, give *me* pleasure without expecting me to do it in return. I *had* done it, today, but I'd wanted to. His cock was magnificent and even now, flaccid and sticky, it was a sight to behold.

"If you want another round, you'll have to give me some more time," he chuckled.

"Wha—that's not—" I flushed red. I hadn't been thinking about more sex, though I wouldn't say no if he offered. "I was just admiring the view," I muttered, not daring to look at him.

That changed his chuckle into a full-out laugh and he stretched out next to me, arms pulling me in close so he could place a chaste kiss on my forehead. "You're sweet."

I didn't like being categorised as *sweet*, but that might be Al's influence, so I kept my mouth shut and went with it. I buried my face in his neck, hooked my arms around neck and rested one leg over his thigh. "So how'd you think I'd be in bed?" I asked in a murmur, taking our conversation back a few steps.

His chest rumbled. "Honestly? I thought you'd be a flustered little virgin."

I snorted. "I'm hardly a virgin. I've been sucking cock for years."

"And this?" He slipped his index finger down my crack, rubbing over my sensitive hole. "You been doing this for years too?"

A moan left me as he slipped the tip of his finger inside me. "N-no. But still not a virgin to it." Wynn was only the second guy to fuck my arse though, the first being Al. The two experiences couldn't be compared though. Not by a long-shot.

Alistair was rough and mostly only wanted to fuck me when I was on my hands and knees. *Maybe so he didn't have to see my flat chest and my dick,* I thought bitterly. *Maybe so he could deceive himself I was actually a girl.* If he didn't have lube nearby, he was happy to settle for spit. Which wasn't ideal—and sometimes it downright hurt.

But Wynn… again, Wynn had only thought of me. He hadn't been rough with me, hadn't fucked just for his own pleasure and not given a rat's arse about mine. No, he'd been fully focused on me the entire time. *That's how it's supposed to be.*

"You're pretty relaxed now." He kissed my temple. "But you're not in the club."

"Well, it's work and it's busy and… yeah, you know." I couldn't tell him people made me nervous, that loud voices were my undoing. That seeing someone who even remotely resembled Alistair made me fumble and drop whatever I held in my hand just from fear it really *was* him.

"No, that's not it." He held me tighter, face nuzzling against my neck. "But I'll stop digging. You're clearly not comfortable talking about it and I don't want you to be anything *but* comfortable in my company."

Oh, I was comfortable with him, all right. A lot more comfortable than I was with anyone else, save maybe Kian and Adam. Mathilda, too, before… but after Al put down the rules I'd withdrawn from her and now she'd buggered off to France as an exchange student.

"Stop it," he said all of a sudden.

"Hmm?"

"You're thinking about something again. Something that makes you tense all over. I don't like it."

That made me chuckle—and the tension he'd noticed creeping in bled back out. "I've never met anyone like you before," I whispered.

"Like me?" He sounded puzzled.

"Someone so kind," I clarified.

He snorted. "Then you've clearly not met many decent people."

Did he categorise himself in the decent people category? Or did he mean he wasn't amongst them? I couldn't tell and I didn't bother asking, because I knew he was a lot more than decent.

"I don't want to get out of bed." He flopped onto his back and dragged me with him to rest on his chest.

"Then don't." I was more than happy to stay like this.

"I dropped the condom on the floor. I should at least throw it in the rubbish before it makes a mess."

So he really is a neat freak. "Leave it. I'll clean it up later." He'd just eaten all our come, so a little of his own seeping onto the floor tiles… I was pretty sure he could handle that.

"Okay," he subsided and that pleased me to no end. Considering how fast he'd cleaned up after breakfast, I'd figured cleaning was his first priority. But I got him to leave the mess on the floor to stay in bed with me, and that… was flattering.

~

I HAD several missed calls from Al and Kian, as well as messages from both of them and Silver. Kian and Silver asked about my audition yesterday and both got more and more worried as I failed to answer, especially the messages from today.

I sent off a quick answer to them. *Didn't get in. Need some time. Sorry.*

Al's messages weren't as easy. At first he'd inquired about the audition too, then said we'd speak when I got home from work in the morning… and then there was a *where-the-hell-are-you* message, followed by veiled threats of what he'd do if he didn't hear from me, if I didn't come home.

"Shit." I swallowed audibly, clutching tight to my phone. I'd pushed him out of my mind all day, deciding to enjoy the good time with Wynn—for as long as it lasted—and face whatever consequences would come later.

I didn't want to though. Not Alistair. I didn't want to face him. I *couldn't*.

"Hey."

I started, head shooting up.

Adam mock-saluted me with a small grin. "What's up with you? You're all pale. Still down about yesterday?" His smile fell as he brought up my botched audition.

I licked my lips. *Adam can help,* a tiny voice whispered in my head. *Adam's a good friend. He'll help you.*

"Kaz?" His brows drew together in a frown.

"I have to talk to you." I didn't know what to *say* though. The whole truth? Only part of the truth? Or just skip all the personal stuff and ask him a favour? "After work?" Our shift was starting soon, after all, and it wouldn't be enough time to speak properly before then.

"Yeah, sure." He studied me closely. "Are you all right?"

I nodded jerkily, even though it was a lie. I didn't want to get into it now, not when we were expected behind the bar in ten minutes. "After work," I repeated, pulling my jumper and T-shirt over my head. I shoved them in my closet and grabbed my workshirt. It was black and form-fitting.

"Hey, Kaz?"

I looked over at Adam to find he had a wicked grin on his lips.

"You got something there." He motioned to his own neck.

I reached up to touch, but couldn't find anything. "What?"

Adam laughed out loud. "Who's going around giving you love-bites?"

Love-bites? I flushed and turned back to bury my head in my closet as I hurried to button up my shirt. It didn't matter if the shirt was buttoned all the way though, because the damn love bite was, apparently, just under my jaw. *Damn you, Wynn! A hickey?* My body liked it—but my brain… now I definitely couldn't go home. Al would flip his shit and I would suffer from it.

"Is he loosening up a bit?" Adam asked then, out of the blue, voice low.

"What?" How'd he know about my wild night and day with Wynn? He couldn't know that!

"Oh, come on, Kaz." Now he just looked exasperated. "I'm not dumb. I know you've had a thing going with Al since back in college. You're not as good at hiding as you think. And moving in together, even with separate bedrooms? *Please.*"

My phone fell to the floor with a loud *crash*. "It's not—you can't—I mean, no, that's not—"

"Hey, Kaz, breathe." Adam was at my side now, patting my shoulder comfortingly. He bent to get my phone and grimaced. "You cracked the screen."

I took the phone with a shaking hand, clutching it tight in case I dropped it again.

"Calm down would you?" He patted my shoulder again, rubbing his hand over my back. "Why is it such a secret? I'm not going to tell anyone."

"You *can't* tell anyone!" My breath came faster, chest rising and falling quickly. "Adam, you can't."

"I said I won't." His frown had deepened.

"And it's not—it's not like that anymore." Alistair didn't know that yet, but I'd been out of love for so long I couldn't fathom what I'd ever seen in him. I just didn't know how to tell him without getting hurt, and I couldn't tell him without having someplace to go. I had to get away first, *then* I could tell him in words.

"It's not?" Adam seemed confused.

I shook my head. "I'll tell you everything after work."

"Okay. Good." He seemed to settle for that, wrapping an arm around my shoulder and squeezing. "I want to tell you to cheer up, but I know that can't be easy for you with a breakup *and* not getting into school." He squeezed my shoulder one last time before letting me go. "If you need a break, whenever, I've got your back, okay?" He winked and walked out.

I stood rooted to the floor, still clutching my phone. He'd got it all wrong. But... I'd tell him. And swear him to secrecy, because if other people found out, Al would *not* be happy. And an unhappy Al usually meant pain for me.

The clock was almost there. I should head out. The screen on my phone didn't just have a little crack, but a big one going all the way down the screen, with lesser ones obscuring the view almost completely.

Dammit. Now I need to splurge for a new phone too. As if I could afford that. Maybe if I bought one of those old types that wasn't a smartphone. Those were cheap nowadays, right? I couldn't spend any money if I had any hopes of finding a flat of my own far away from Alistair.

And I had to. I had to get away from him. Even if I had to live in a run-down shack. But hopefully Adam would let me crash for a little while. They had a guest-room, after all, and if I offered to pay some rent...

Please Adam.

I squeezed my eyes shut, shut my locker, took several deep breaths... then I walked out to face a crowded, loud club, hoping tonight would be a better one than yesterday had been. I didn't hold out any hope for it, however.

CHAPTER 5

I couldn't do it. My head wasn't in the game. Even if it had been, it was too overwhelming. Too many people, too loud, too many raised voices. The knowledge that Adam knew about Alistair and me, and what Al would do when he found out— and it was a when, because he *always* found out—had me on the verge of a nervous breakdown.

"Go take a break." Adam pushed me away from the bar.

I should stay, insist I was fine and able to do my job, but I wasn't and I didn't. I bolted for the back room, the breakdown in full progress as I ran. By the time I was safely in the deserted back room, the tears streamed freely.

I'm such a failure. I can't do anything right! And if I

went home I'd suffer for it. Suffer for crying, for botching my audition, for being such an emotional wreck… and worst of all, I'd suffer for Adam knowing even if I'd never told him or even hinted at it.

"I'm getting a feeling of deja vú, except we're inside and it's not raining."

I lowered my hands to look up at Wynn. He was blurry because of my tears, but that didn't take anything away from his appearance. He leant against the doorway, arms crossed over his chest, dark gaze on me.

"I'm s-sorry!" I covered my face again, unable to let him look at what a wreck I was. I wished he'd just leave, let me fall apart in private. "I c-can't do this! This j-j-job—I'm n-not a-any good a-at it!"

He sighed heavily—then walked across the floor and wrapped me up in his strong arms.

I froze, surprised. But he only held me and I succumbed to it, leaning against him, crying against his chest. His grip around me was tight, his head rested on top of mine, and he pushed me up against the lockers.

He didn't ask questions. He didn't say *anything*. He simply held me while I cried and he continued to do so as I slowly calmed down. I'd kept my hands over my face even as I cried on him, but now I slowly lowered them and wrapped my arms around his waist.

My breathing was shaky, but at least the tears and sobs had stopped for now. It was all thanks to him, his calming presence not demanding answers or degrading me.

"There you go." He took a step back and wiped his hands over my face. "Do you feel a little better now?"

Better? Hardly. But at least I felt like I wasn't falling apart by the seams anymore. That had to count for something. "Y-yeah."

He didn't let go of my face, instead he cupped his palms over my cheeks and leaned in to press a brief, chaste kiss to my lips. They probably tasted salty from my tears, but he didn't comment. "You're gonna go home now, Kasey—"

I started shaking my head furiously before he'd even finished. The thought of going home was part of the reason I'd broken down in the first place and I *couldn't.*

"Yes, you are." His thumbs stroked over my cheeks, then he let me go and reached into his pocket. I only closed my eyes, trying not to let the waterworks run lose, until a jingling of keys made me blink them open again. "Here." He pressed the keys into my hand, folding my fingers over them. "Go home. Take a shower, go to sleep, watch TV, whatever makes you feel good. I'll take over here and I'll be home once I close the club."

My lips parted, but no words came. He wanted me to go back to his place? He was trusting me with his keys? I stared down at them. "What if I rob you?" was all I could think about saying, silently chastising myself for letting something so stupid out.

He chuckled. "Well, I know your name and I know where you work, so…"

I drew in a shaky breath, tightening my grip around the keys. "I don't mean to be such a bother. I don't—I'm—"

"It's okay." He put both hands on my shoulders, squeezing gently. "Not everyone's made out for this kind of work. We'll figure it out, okay? But for now, you go home and I'll take over for you here."

I bowed my head, ashamed and grateful all at once.

"This your locker?" Wynn had moved off to the side and opened the door as soon as I nodded. "What happened to your phone?" He frowned down at the cracked screen.

"Dropped it," I muttered, shame washing over me again. I could never do anything right.

He was in front of me, fingers unbuttoning my shirt deftly. I dared a quick glance up, but he was intent on his task. When it was unbuttoned all the way he slid it down my arms and off, throwing it into my locker before coming back with my T-shirt. It felt weird for him to dress me, but I didn't object, just lifted my arms.

Once my T-shirt and jumper were on, he moved behind me to help me put my jacket on.

"I can dress myself, you know," I murmured, not sure if I should be embarrassed or grateful he seemed to care enough to help.

"I know." He wrapped his arms around my shoulders from behind, hugging me close. I leaned into him, turning my head so my nose rubbed against his neck. "Feel at home, okay? Do whatever you want."

I gazed up at him. "I'll wait up for you."

He grinned wryly, reaching up to tilt my head up further. "I'd like that." He kissed me briefly, then let go and stepped back, reaching into my locker again and handing me my phone. "But I won't mind if you can't either."

I watched him for a moment. His tall, fit body, the tattoos that showed over the hem of his shirt. His black hair, shaved on the sides and longer on top, styled perfectly. His dark eyes, angular face, slight stubble, how his lower lip was plumper than his top. And his ears, with several piercings in each. I wanted to continue watching him; or even better, I wanted to have him stretched out naked under me so I could look at every inch of skin, memorise all his tattoos, make him feel as good as he'd made me feel.

He stepped closer, still with that wry grin. "When I get home tonight." He pressed his thumb to my lips.

"If you're awake, I'll rim you so good you won't be able to even remember your name."

I swallowed audibly—and blood ran south at the mental images his words brought forth. "I'll be awake." Oh, would I ever. I'd never been rimmed before, but I'd seen it in porn, and well... guys who got rimmed seemed to enjoy it immensely.

"Go home." He pushed me gently backwards, thumb moving from my lips down to caress my jaw. "Don't worry about this place. Okay?"

"Okay," I agreed meekly, though the club was the least of my problems.

He gave me another kiss, this one long, drawn-out —then pushed me out into the hallway and gave me a light shove in the direction of the backdoor. He watched me go, and when I was at the door, pushing the handle down, I glanced back. He smiled, a real smile this time, then turned and headed into the club proper.

It wasn't until I was halfway to his flat that I remembered I'd arranged to have a chat with Adam after work. And my phone was too cracked to write out a message to him. *Shit*. I hoped Wynn would come up with a good excuse. Or the truth, for that matter. He seemed like the sort of guy who'd tell the truth. And I wouldn't mind if he did—I was done being someone's dirty little secret.

～

IN THE END, I didn't manage to stay awake. I browsed through Wynn's Netflix—he had a big, flatscreen SmartTV—found *Footloose*, the original, not the remake, and settled down on the sofa to watch. The sofa was soft, Footloose was familiar, and it lulled me to sleep sometime after the brilliant warehouse dance.

I woke briefly to Wynn scooping me up into his arms. I sighed happily, slung one arm over his shoulder, and dozed back off as he carried me to bed. I didn't even remember him setting me down again or snuggle up next to me—but when I woke up it was to daylight streaming in the window and a big, hard body spooned to my back.

Speaking of hard... something else hard lay against the small of my back. He was breathing deeply though, so he was clearly still asleep.

I fumbled blindly at the nightstand, found my phone and brought it over to check the time. Except it wasn't my phone, but his. His screen was all shiny and looked new, not a single crack in it. I shouldn't snoop on his phone, but I'd already pressed the home button as I grabbed it, and the clock showed up.

Only nine. I yawned, put his phone back on the nightstand, and relaxed back against him. He was warm, arm heavy around my waist, breath warm on my neck. *Fuck, but this is how it's supposed to be like when you're with someone*. This was what I'd dreamt about. Sleeping curled up with someone, waking up spooned together, lazing around in bed, or taking care of morning boners.

Would he like it if I woke him up with a blowjob? I had no idea, so I didn't dare do it, but that would definitely be hot. And the rim-job he'd promised me... my dick ached at the thought of experiencing that.

I dozed for a while but my bladder eventually made itself known, and I wriggled out of his arms to tip-toe over the floor to the bathroom. I took a piss, washed my hands, and brushed my teeth—with the new toothbrush he'd handed me yesterday. Then I took a proper look at myself in the mirror... and spotted the hickey Adam had pointed out.

Damn. It sure showed. Weird no one else had commented on it. But then I wasn't friends with any of my other co-workers, so maybe not. I fingered my bruised skin thoughtfully. This had been bruised in *pleasure*, not by Alistair backhanding me or pushing me into furniture. This truly was a *love-bite*, as Adam had so nicely called it. I didn't mind it at all.

I took a quick shower, just to be on the safe side. When he woke... if he still wanted to do what he'd promised me last night, I had to be ready for it.

Once done, I started to tip-toe back into the

bedroom again, only to find Wynn on his back and awake. His head turned my way, eyes having a strange pull on me as I walked to the bed. "Morning," I whispered.

His lips tilted up. "Come here, Kasey. I believe I promised you something last night."

Oh! He was going to do it. His dick, which I'd felt pressed against my upper arse and lower back earlier, curved nicely upwards, showing off the piercings. The head was flushed red, a drop of pre-come glinting at his slit.

He grabbed my hand and pulled me onto the bed. "Don't you want it?" he asked, eyebrows raised.

"Yes!" I flushed, but moved eagerly closer. "How do you want me?"

"On your stomach." He pushed up on his elbows and I stretched out, holding the pillow over my arms and resting my head atop it. "Yeah, exactly like that." He rolled over to straddle my ankles, then his hands were on my arse cheeks, kneading gently, parting them to reveal my hole.

I didn't know what to expect, but I tried to relax. I moved my legs a little further apart so he'd have more space, and he rewarded that by running a finger down my crack, rubbing at my hole.

The mattress moved with him as he lay down too and he pulled my arse cheeks apart again. Then his tongue licked over my hole and I forgot to breathe. The fact I buried my face in the pillow didn't help either, but damn—that was something else.

He licked over my hole again, tongue warm and slicked with spit. I rocked against him lightly, not daring to do it too much in case he didn't want a face-full of arse, but enough so his tongue pressed harder against my entrance. He took the hint, pushing the tip inside.

I strangled a groan, grabbing onto the sheets for dear life. My dick had started to leak under me, creating a wet spot, but that didn't matter at all right now as long as he kept his tongue in my arse.

He pushed in and out, alternating with licking up my crack and over my hole, then pushing in again.

My nerve endings were on *fire*. My dick was ready to blow. *I did* not *know it was possible to come from being rimmed*. In porn they did, but in porn they could come from anything. I hadn't imagined I would be so into having my arse licked, though. But here I was, on the verge of orgasm.

Wynn pulled away, flipped me over as easily as if I weight nothing, pushed my thighs up, and then he dove back in again. I groaned low in my throat, threw one arm over my eyes, and let the other hand find my cock. I stroked myself quickly, *so damn close* and needing to reach my orgasm *now*.

Something between a cry and a sob left me as I came, making a right mess of my stomach.

"So it's safe to say you liked it?" He sat back on his knees, grinning down at me.

I gazed up at him, lips parted. I slowly lowered my legs down on the bed, the muscles protesting a little at being held up and away until now. "You think?" My chest rose and fell quickly. I looked at his dick, it was still hard, still curved upwards, head flushed, pre-come leaking. "Come up here and you can fuck my mouth."

His eyes narrowed a fraction. "Yeah?"

"Yeah." He'd given me a rim-job, I'd let him fuck my mouth. I didn't think he'd go so far as to stuff my mouth with his dick to the point I nearly choked, like Al liked to do. No, Wynn was a lot more considerate, a lot more in tune with my needs.

He straddled my chest, braced his hands against the wall, and pushed his hips forward. His cock-head nudged my lips and I parted them, sucking it in, the salty pre-come spreading on my tongue. He stopped, letting me suck on only his head. He didn't start to move again until I loosened my jaw and gazed up at him in silence.

His stomach muscles tensed as he tried to restrain himself, but then he started thrusting forward. He didn't go too hard and not too far back, but he thrust quickly. Spit mixed with his pre-come trickled from my lower lip, the only way it could go when I was unable to swallow.

He leant further against the wall, bracing his forearms against it, and continued to thrust his hips. At one point he thrust a little too far down my throat, but he pulled back before I could gag and he didn't do it again.

"Can I come in your mouth?" he asked then, voice deep and hoarse.

I made a sound, but it didn't sound like either a yes or a no, so instead I gave him a thumbs' up. And just like that, he came—filling my mouth with thick, sticky sperm. Some of it stuck to his dick as he pulled back and I swallowed the rest, then licked my lips to make sure I got it all. I also wiped spit, pre-come and semen off my chin, as some had trickled there. Then I grabbed his hips, pulled him back in, and sucked the rest of it off his softening cock.

"Fuck," he groaned.

He collapsed beside me, sweat beading his temples and over his chest. I ran my hand over his chest, through the smattering of dark, coarse hair and over both his nipples. I kissed the one closest to me before moving up to brush my lips over his stubbly jaw.

"God, I want to kiss you." But instead of doing just that, he pushed up and off the bed. "I'm gonna brush my teeth first." He winked as he walked off.

Considering he'd just had his mouth in my arse, brushing his teeth was likely a good idea. Even I was a bit squicky at the thought of kissing after rimming, but that wasn't to say I didn't want to try it myself. *Wonder if he ever wants to switch places?*

He came back out with a damp washcloth that he proceeded to wash off my stomach with. Like the neat freak he was, he walked back to the bathroom with it to deposit it before he finally came back to bed.

But then his lips attached to mine and we rolled over until I was draped over him. And we kissed, and kissed, and kissed. I didn't ever want to stop. He was the best thing to ever have happened to me—and considering it was only our second day together, that said a lot.

CHAPTER 6

"*D*oes the job really make you that miserable?"

I opened my eyes and turned my head to look at him. He was stretched out on his back next to me, arms hooked under his head as he stared up at the ceiling. I'd been dozing pleasantly, but now he'd brought last night back to me, my mood soured quickly.

"It's not just the job. It's other things too. Like my audition." And Al, the worst of it. But how could I tell Wynn I was technically still in a relationship? Not that it was much of one... and Al was the one who'd wanted to have an open relationship in the first place— but that was mostly on his own part, so he could keep sleeping around with girls whenever he started feeling too gay.

His eyes crinkled a little in thought. "I can help you find a new job, if you like."

"I don't know what I'd do. I'm not good at anything," I murmured, but my chest warmed at his offer.

"Surely that's not true. You're aspiring to get into a dance school, so you're good at dancing, at least."

"Not good enough." There wasn't really anything I could do. Al told me so all the time. "I guess... I'm good at sex." Al had never had much to complain about there, anyway, but then again he was only after his own pleasure.

Wynn snorted. "So what? Prostitution?"

I chuckled darkly. "Nah, I don't think that would work well for me either."

"Why not?" he prodded gently.

I had to think about how to answer that one. "Because you never know what kind of people you'll end up having to sleep with, I guess."

"If you ever decide to do that, I'll pay you a living wage just to have sex with me. Only me," he said, and I was pretty sure it was a joke. He seemed more than a little serious though. Then he asked, "Has someone ever hurt you?"

And now everything got serious. "Why do you ask that?"

"Answer the question, Kasey." And *that* was an order.

I'd planned on telling Adam last night, because Adam was my friend and I knew he'd help. Hopefully he'd let me stay with him and his boyfriend too. But Wynn... Judging from what I'd learned the past two days, he *would* help me. But was that wise? We didn't know each other, he was my boss, we weren't in any kind of official relationship.

"Yes," I whispered, my voice barely carrying—but he heard it.

His voice was tight when he spoke next. "Who?"

I licked my lips nervously and sat up, slouching a little as I stared down at the sheets. "You have to let me explain."

"Explain what?"

I didn't dare look at him, but his voice was still tight, reined in. "Back in college I fancied this guy. He was one of the best friends of *my* best friend. Mathilda and I—we danced together. That's how I know her. And Alistair, he was in her class, a good friend. And he was handsome and I *really* liked him. I think I was a little obsessive about it, actually." I'd been a fool. "He noticed it anyway and started showing up whenever I was alone. We snuck off together because he wanted his dick sucked. I... did it. Every time he wanted me to. But he never did it back."

I clenched my hands, hating how pathetic I sounded. Why hadn't I understood it back then? "I thought I was in love. I understood it was hard for him to come out to his friends and his family. So we were together—but in secret." I hated secrecy. But now I was pretty sure I hated Al more. "When he finished school and started university he suggested we live together. As flatmates—with each our bedroom, sharing rent. I… I moved in with him. I was *happy* he wanted to live with me. That meant what we had was actually special, you know?" *Stupid, stupid, stupid.* "That maybe he was working up to coming out. But then, after I'd moved in, he said he wanted an open relationship. And I agreed, because I didn't want to lose him. We were young, after all, and like he said, lots of gay couples are in open relationships."

I just sounded more and more pathetic. I didn't dare glance down at Wynn, who was still lying down, unmoving. And what he said about open relationships… I didn't know anyone in that sort of situation. Kian and Silver were monogamous, as far as I knew, as were Adam and his boyfriend. And they'd been together for years too, ever since college.

"It turned out he wanted to sleep with women. When he wanted his dick sucked or he fancied a piece of arse, then I was good enough. But only for a fuck, nothing more, *ever*. He never… reciprocated." And that hurt, because when you loved someone you'd want to give them pleasure too, right? "And then he slapped me. I don't even remember what for. I just… he continued doing that whenever he wasn't happy with me. He'd slap me around, or shove me, or yell at me. Saying I was never good enough, I could never do anything right. And he *was* right, because I can't. I mess everything up."

Wynn moved, the mattress shifting a little. He'd sat up, braced on one hand, while the other rested on his bent knee. "Where is that arsehole now?"

"At home," I whispered, bending over, breath coming in quick spurts. "And he's gonna be so angry with me for being gone for so long and for not letting him know. I don't want to go home, I don't want to face him, I don't want to be with him… but I've got nowhere to go. Kian knows we're together and he'll want to know why if I move back in with them. He likes Al, he's not going to believe the truth. He's going to believe *him*." I pressed my hands to my mouth, fighting tears.

Wynn rubbed my back soothingly. "Don't have a panic attack now, okay? There's no need for that."

I squeezed my eyes shut. "I don't know what to do. I was going to work for a year to save up for school and a place of my own, but now there's no school, and

I can't even do my job properly. And my phone's broken and I can't afford a new one, and—"

"Hey, *shhh*." He hugged me close, still stroking his hand over my back. "I said no panic attack. This is all easily fixed."

Easily fixed? Well, wasn't he a ray of sunshine and rainbows. I'd been struggling with this *forever*. It wasn't easily fixed at all.

"If there's one thing I hate, it's abusive arseholes like him. You really want to move out of there? Get away from him?"

I nodded.

"Do you have a lot of stuff?"

"Well, the flat came furnished, so… just clothes and stuff." Stuff was a lot, actually. Books and electronic equipment and an extensive DVD collection.

"Then I'll help you," he said, like I'd half-hoped, half-expected, because he was *that* kind. "So no need for panic attacks. I'll help you get your stuff. And if I meet that fucker, *his* face will be introduced to *my* fist."

I had a feeling that perhaps him saying that should unnerve me… but it didn't. If anything, it made me feel even safer with him. Maybe that was stupid—two days in, to trust someone so much—but he had been nothing but kind. Alistair had never treated me like Wynn did, not even in the beginning.

"As for a place to stay… you can stay here if you

want." His hand cupped my neck, thumb rubbing circles over my skin. "I know we haven't talked about *this* between us, but I'm not usually a one-off kind of guy."

Considering he'd watched me for months, and hadn't ever planned on so much as speaking to me, I'd already suspected as much. "But two days in... Isn't that a little too hasty? That's the sort of thing that happens in song and films and novels."

He chuckled. "Sometimes real life can be even more incredible than the most cliché song or film or novel. But I'm not forcing you. I'm just giving you an option. If you feel you can't go back to your brother, my door's open for you."

I leaned into him, tucking my head in the nook where his neck met his shoulder. "I used to think I'd done something really horrible in a previous life, but now... I must've done something right, to meet someone like you."

He enveloped me further in his arms, squeezing me close. "If you want, we can get this done right away. The quicker you get out of that flat, the quicker you get him out of your life."

There was nothing I wanted more than to not have to deal with Alistair anymore. "He should be at university until four o'clock at least." Al always had long days, but then he was studying engineering, so I reckoned that went with the territory. Add to that the travel home and he didn't have much free time when homework and studying was factored in.

I dreaded going back to the flat, though. Dreaded what would meet me. But if Wynn came with me... I was safe. He'd protect me. Alistair had nothing to Wynn's physique—Wynn could probably flatten him with one hit. Knowing that made me a little braver too and I squared my shoulders as I sat up and away from him. "Let's do it."

Wynn nodded, the wry grin in place, but his usually expressionless face seeming somewhat... satisfied.

~

WHAT HAD LOOMED AHEAD of me as sort of horror turned out to be anything but. Alistair wasn't home, so we got my stuff packed and into the car Wynn had managed to borrow from someone. As Wynn hefted the last bag with DVDs, I went into the kitchen and ripped a blank page of the small notepad hanging on the fridge.

I wrote *It's over* on that blank paper, stuck it to the fridge with a magnet, and took a step back to look at it. Should I write more? But no, Alistair didn't deserve any more than that.

If he'd really wanted to be with me, he would've treated me differently. He wouldn't have lied and been both physically and emotionally abusive. He would've been more like Wynn, taking care of me and making sure I was happy too.

So Wynn and I went on our way without meeting Al. We didn't meet anyone, not even any neighbours.

Carrying all my stuff up to his flat was another matter. Al's flat had been on the ground floor—Wynn's was on the top floor. But we lugged it all up and Wynn stacked everything against one living room wall. It was rather neat, nothing out of place.

"I have to return the car. Do you want to come with me or stay here?"

I'd worried so much about getting my stuff I was emotionally drained. "Do you mind if I stay here?" All I wanted was to curl up on the sofa or the bed and let it sink in that I didn't have to go back to Al anymore. That all my stuff was here and there was nothing for me there.

"Of course not." He ran his fingers through my hair and planted a chaste kiss on my forehead. "I'll be back soon."

He left and I ambled over the sofa. My phone, cracked screen and all, lay on the table. I pressed the home button, saw I had a missed call and could just barely make out it was from Adam through the cracks.

I could probably manage to ring him back, but I didn't want to do this over the phone. And I couldn't send a message.

I decided to ring him back. I'd vanished on him last night, after all, so it was only decent to do.

"Kaz!" he answered. "There you are. What the hell happened last night? Wynn said he sent you home. Are you in trouble?"

"Ahh, no, no I'm not." His barrage of words startled me. "I just had a really bad day. I'm better now." Loads better now my biggest worry was out of the world. "I'll tell you all about it, but not over the phone. How about tomorrow?"

"Why not today before work?"

"I don't work today." Thankfully, as I wasn't sure I could face another night of a crowded, noisy nightclub in my frazzled state. "But how about lunch tomorrow? We could go to Harriet's? Around one? Or two, if that's better?"

He laughed. "Two, I think. I work all night, after all, and I damn well plan on spending most of my morning asleep."

"That's what I figured," I chuckled. "I wanted to send you a message last night, but my screen—well, you saw it yourself. I'm lucky I can even see enough of the screen to call people."

"Yeah, you ruined that one pretty good," he

conceded. "You could probably get the screen fixed though. I don't think that's too expensive."

"Yeah?" I perked up at that. "I'll look into it. Thanks, Adam."

"Anytime, Kaz. So, two tomorrow at Harriet's, right?"

"Yep." It was pretty much our standard meeting place for lunch. His brother had worked there when he was younger, both before and after he started culinary school, and now he manned the kitchen full-time.

"See you tomorrow!" Adam hung up after that cheerful goodbye.

I stared at my screen, for once not really seeing the cracks. Adam sounded *really* cheerful. Maybe he'd just got laid. I didn't think he saw much of his own boyfriend lately, what with him at university during the day and Adam working nights.

For once I could actually be happy for Adam, happy that he was happy, instead of that happiness mixed in with jealousy. I was done with my abusive relationship, and… a new, normal one might just lie ahead of me.

Shit. Going straight from one relationship to another. Was there a word for that? It felt like there should be, if it wasn't. What would people say? Not that that mattered, not really, but… Kian didn't care for Wynn, I knew that much. What would he say when he found out? He was my brother after all, and if anyone's opinions mattered, it was his.

I dozed on the sofa, contemplating Kian's reaction, trying to figure out what to say if he reacted with this or that.

Wynn came home eventually, after over an hour away. "Here." He dropped something on my stomach.

I started, not expecting *that*. I sat up, took the little bag, and held it up. "What's this?"

"Look for yourself." He nodded at it, then turned and walked around the kitchen counter to the fridge. If he was actually looking for something or if he was giving me space I had no idea.

I peeked into the bag… and my jaw dropped. "But —Wynn! This is too expensive!"

"You need it, don't you?" he countered with.

"Yes, but—not the newest model! I didn't even need a smartphone, really, just one I can text with." Because yes, inside the bag was a brand new phone— same brand as the one I had, but at least two models newer. And probably costing twice as much.

"Look." He turned around and put his hands on the counter, leaning forward a little. "You needed a new phone. I bought one for you. Think of it like a… I don't know, housewarming gift or something."

"People don't buy brand new smartphones for a housewarming gift," I murmured, but the phone beckoned me. It had a better camera, better space on it, more apps I could use. "I'll pay you back."

"No need. Kasey, I've got the money. Don't worry about it." He came over to plop down next to me on the sofa, where he proceeded to grab my hand and twine our fingers together. "I've got my own business that's doing quite well. I've got my flat and everything else I need. I don't spend a lot of money—but I wanted to buy this for you. And I didn't splurge for no reason —you did need a new phone after all."

I bit my lower lip. I still thought it was too expensive a gift, but he didn't seem to think so and no matter what I said I didn't think I'd get him to change his mind. "Thank you." I leaned in and up, tilting my head just so.

He understood—dipping his own for a kiss. Best to go with it, but if this turned into a habit... no way. I'd be really careful with this new phone so I didn't drop it anywhere.

"And you say you're not a nice person," I mumbled, eyes half-closed as we kissed again. "That's the biggest lie I've ever heard."

He grinned against my lips. "Only when it comes to you."

How was I supposed to resist such flattering words? *Easy; I don't.*

CHAPTER 7

a few hours before the club was supposed to open, Wynn dragged me down there to teach me to mix drinks himself. I hadn't had the best training, only learning the standard menu, and all training had happened while on the clock, with a full club and people ordering continuously.

But being in the club with only Wynn, when it was light out and completely empty... that was something else altogether.

The guy who'd taught me had slapped the drink menu in front of me, told me to memorise it, and then I'd been thrown behind the bar. Adam always helped me out when I worked with him, and Cooper too to some degree, but the sheer number of drinks easily overwhelmed me.

Add to the fact that we didn't just make drinks on the menu, but whatever drink people wanted as long as we had the right ingredients, and it was all a mess in my head.

But with Wynn as my teacher, I didn't do half bad. Wynn was good at this, to the point he could even do some fancy throws with the bottles that I was never going to attempt.

"I've got a rule," Wynn was saying as he mixed a fancy-looking drink. "If someone orders a drink that's not on the main menu, and I'm unsure, I always dip a straw in to taste it. If it's not right, it's best to put it aside and mix a new one. Better that than getting complaints." He sat four glasses in front of me, two regular glasses, the other two cocktail glasses. "Now, take a sip of all four. These are four of the drinks we get asked for the most that are not on the main menu."

I wasn't that fond of alcohol, but I dutifully did as he told me to. Three of the four tasted nasty, but the fourth wasn't so bad.

He grinned. "I'll teach you these four, then you're going to mix every single drink on the regular menu for me."

My eyes widened. "All of them? But..." I glanced behind me at the shelf of bottles. "Isn't that going to be expensive? Wasting all that alcohol simply for me to learn to mix them all?"

"I wouldn't do this for every employee, true. But for you it'll be worth it."

It was both flattering and disconcerting.

He leaned against the counter, watching me carefully. "You're too nervous, that's your problem. So, we're going to nail all the regular drinks so they're stuck in there." He tapped my head gently. "If you're confident about the drinks, about how to make them and that they'll taste good, you'll be more comfortable behind the bar, yeah? And only when you know the recipes from heart, then you can start working on mixing them faster."

I nodded my understanding and he set to work, but not mixing the drinks again. No, this time I was the one mixing them while he simply told me what to do. "It's easier to put it to memory when you do the work yourself," as he said, and it was true. It was so with dancing too. Simply watching a choreography wasn't enough to learn it, I had to go through it myself, using my own body to learn every single move.

"I think you've got these four now. I'll go do some paperwork while you work on all the other drinks, okay? Come get me when you're done."

He was going to leave me alone? Then again, I had the menu in front of me, so it wasn't like I *needed* his expertise when it came to these. I'd mixed them countless times in the months I'd worked here, so this was all about properly putting them to memory. "Can we turn on some music?" It was weird being all alone in the bar, facing the big, empty room with no sound but the ones I made myself.

"Sure. I'll put the radio on." He ran a hand through my hair, kissed my temple, and walked off. Not long after, music filled the club. It wasn't the regular dance, electro, techno music that blasted from the speakers, but radio edits of popular songs.

I smiled to myself as I perused the menu in front of me. *Mojito.* That one was ordered *often.* I set to work, trying to mix from memory, but frequently had to check the menu because I'd forgotten something or because I just wanted to be sure. I took actual sips of the drinks now too, since these were only for me anyway, putting the tastes to mind.

Then one of my favourite songs started playing. *Lights* by Ellie Goulding—Mathilda and I had choreographed a dance to that one just this summer, before she left for France and before I mostly cut her off from my life. I missed her, and I missed dancing with her, and choreographing in general. I'd been so busy with work and getting ready for my audition that I hadn't danced for fun in ages.

The club was enormous, with lots of space now it wasn't filled with people writhing together on the dance floor. I couldn't help myself. Wynn was in his office, so I was all alone. No one would see me.

I moved out onto the dance floor, a bit hesitant, but the music washed over me and I could see the moves Mathilda and I had spent endless hours working out in my mind and then more hours practicing to get it just right.

My body moved on its own. The song had only reached the middle, but that didn't matter. I knew the moves well enough to start anywhere. It felt freeing to simply dance for myself again, without an audience to judge me, or for a performance through school or my old dance studio. It was just me and the music. No one to impress.

The song ended and smoothly changed into Kelly Clarkson's *Stronger*, and though I didn't have moves choreographed for that one, I was quite good at improvisation when I was in the zone. Besides, that was also one of my favourite songs, I didn't even stop to think about it.

That was, until the end of the song and I caught a glimpse of Wynn leaning against the bar, and I stumbled to a halt. "How long've you been standing there?"

"Long enough." He studied me. "Do you have social anxiety?"

He'd startled me and my breathing was quick and he'd just watched me dance without saying a word and

—*argh*. I flushed in embarrassment. "Are you a therapist?" I shot back in a murmur.

He chuckled. "Hardly. But I've seen my fair share of them. Social anxiety isn't a laughing matter. Or did that arsehole ex of yours simply beat all self-confidence out of you?"

I tangled my fingers nervously, not sure how to answer that. It was true that people made me nervous, that I made mistakes when there were others around or when I was stressed. That I didn't like to be in big crowds. But... had I always been like that? I'd used to be confident about my dancing, way back before when Mathilda and I were tight and I'd discovered just how Alistair really was. But I'd always been shy too and not very good at performing well when it mattered.

He was in front of me now, hand running through my hair. *He's grown fond of that. He did it earlier too.* I looked up, meeting his gaze. His eyes flickered between mine. "It's probably the last one, isn't it?" His lips flattened. "I swear if I ever meet that guy—"

I threw my arms around his neck and hugged him tight. "Thank you. For everything. You don't even really know me and yet you've done so much for me."

"Yeah, well..." Now *he* sounded embarrassed. "You're a great dancer, you know. You only stumbled once you realised I was watching you. Before that you did wonderfully."

I wasn't sure I quite believed that, but I went with it, burying my face in his neck instead of arguing about it. "Wynn?"

"Hmm?" His hands splayed over my back.

"Are you gay?" This worried me a little. Alistair always told me he was bi, but to everyone else he was straight, and just... I didn't want to be in another relationship where the person I was with also wanted to be with other people. Not that being gay, if he was, would exclude that—lots of gay people were in open relationships too, but... I didn't make any sense. Still, the question burned.

He full out laughed. "I've been shagging you for two days, haven't I?"

"Yeah, but," I mumbled, "you could be bi."

"Kasey." He grabbed my shoulder and pushed me away, holding me at arms' length. "I'm a hundred percent gay. Trust me. I've never had any interest in women. Hell, I've hardly ever had any interest in men either, so it's safe to say I'm pretty monogamous."

It was like he'd read my thoughts. "But you've had some interest in guys?"

He grimaced briefly—but I caught it, because I was already staring at him. "I had a boyfriend. Years ago. And... I used to sleep with my best friend before he shacked up with his two lovers. But... that's it, basically. There's been a couple people, but they weren't all that important in the end."

Two lovers? Open relationship? Or no… Kian had a friend who had two boyfriends—and the boyfriends were together too. They were in a monogamous relationship, the three of them. And wasn't that how Kian knew of Wynn? Through that guy…

"What happened to your boyfriend?" If he'd been so important, why wasn't Wynn with him? Maybe he'd broken his heart.

Wynn let his hands drop from my shoulders as he turned to head back to the bar. "He died."

Oh shit. "I'm sorry."

"Nothing for you to be sorry for." He started tasting the drinks I'd mixed. "He killed himself. Left a note and everything. That's the only reason I didn't end up doing prison time."

I walked up to the front of the bar, leaning against it as I watched him take healthy swallows from each glass. "Prison time?"

He glanced up briefly. "They were my drugs."

Oh. Drugs… Was he still—

"Don't worry," he interrupted my thoughts. "I don't deal drugs anymore. Stopped after… well, *that*. Like I said, it's years ago. Now I've got all this." He spread his arms wide to indicate the club. "I've got a good life."

"What about family?" He'd already started this topic of conversation, so I felt safe asking, prodding to find out more about him.

He made a decidedly bitter sound. "I don't have any family. None that wants to have anything to do with me, anyway. I've got my club. My flat. A best friend."

That sounded sad. Then again, I didn't even have *that*. I didn't have my own place to live, didn't have a job I liked, had pushed away my best friend... I still had Adam though. And I had my family, even if I hadn't spoken to them in a while.

Mum and Dad didn't live in London anymore, so I didn't get to see them all that often. Kian and Silver... well, they had their own life to live. I should at least tell them I'd moved, but they'd want to know where, and I still didn't dare ask Wynn if he wanted this to get out. This thing between us...

"These are good." He sat down the last glass. It clinked against the counter. "Did you have a taste?" When I nodded he asked, "What'd you think?"

"I'm not that fond of alcohol, really."

He chuckled and picked a glass at random, tipping it to his lips. "I probably shouldn't start drinking overly much either. I did, after—well, it was a really bad time in my life, but I got over it." I swear there was an *eventually* tacked onto the end there, to go along with his bittersweet smile. "Anyway. Do you want to mix these again? Or do you want to get out of here?"

"No, that's okay. I think I've got it. I can practice a little more tomorrow before work, maybe." I walked around the counter to him.

He glanced at me, then drew me into his arms. I hooked mine around his neck, and his hands cupped my arse... and next thing I knew he'd lifted me up to sit on the counter, showing all the half-empty glasses off to the side. His lips claimed mine, soft, cold from the drinks he'd had, the taste of them a mix of the drinks—vodka, rum, Coke, gin...

"If it's been so long since your boyfriend died and you used to sleep with your friend," I started breathlessly. "Then why me now?"

"I don't know." His hands ran down my sides and under my thighs, lifting them so I could wrap my legs properly around his hips. "The day you started here... I saw you come out of the back room with Adam, looking all kinds of nervous. I haven't been able to stop looking at you since."

My heart did a sudden jump and I clutched harder at him, tilting my head away so he'd move his lips further down my neck.

"Say, Kasey..." He sucked on the thin skin beneath my jaw—on the opposite side of the last hickey he'd made on me. "Why aren't you afraid of me? Most people are. Or they just don't like me. I can be very direct. And rude. And I don't have very much patience with much of anything."

I closed my eyes, rocking my hips against his slightly. "Maybe that's true for other people, but you're not like that with me. You watched me for so long without saying anything and when you didn't have a choice but to speak to me, you were so kind and compassionate. You're not rude to me—and you have endless patience with me."

He chuckled, lips sliding downwards. "I guess you're special then. But really... I saw you, and you seemed nervous then about starting a new job, and every time after that I saw you... you were all nerves, eyes going wide the minute someone spoke to you, like you were afraid they'd hurt you. I guess that tugged at me. I don't like seeing people so afraid all the time. No one should go around and constantly be afraid."

I didn't know I'd seemed like that to other people. I'd thought I was good at keeping it hidden. *Obviously not.* Wynn had seen it—and he hadn't even known me. "Then why stay away?"

"Because I know what people say about me. I didn't want to make you feel even worse. I mean, if Cooper can get you to look like a deer caught in headlights, I didn't even want to think about what you'd feel about me."

"Cooper?" Cooper was... he was very sexual. He seemed to get along great with Adam—at least at work. I didn't know if they hung out outside of work or anything. Cooper was flirty and it had surprised me. He was very open about his sexuality and his sex life, and having lived with Al for so long where everything was a secret... yeah, Cooper had been a bit of a shock.

"Yeah, Cooper... He asked Adam about you. If you were single." He nipped at my lower lip now. "And Adam told him you were, but that he was to stay away from you."

"Why?" Why was Adam warning Cooper away from me? Not that I had any interest in Cooper... he was handsome and all, but he was someone who definitely wouldn't be able to keep his dick in his pants.

"Hell if I know." He grabbed my hips and pulled me flush up against him, his half-hard dick rubbing against mine. "He just told him to get his rocks off elsewhere and leave you alone."

Maybe because Adam had already known about Al? Even if he hadn't got it confirmed...

"I think he was trying to protect you. Cooper's a bit of a slag, after all." He chuckled again, chest rumbling. "But I'm not. A slag that is. I like to think I'm pretty loyal."

My breath caught in my throat. "I am too, I think," I whispered.

"What a pair we make." He rubbed our noses together and dragged his lips over mine.

I chuckled, still sort of breathless. "I'm so hard right now." That hadn't exactly been what I'd meant to say, but it was true. My dick strained against my skinny jeans.

His usual wry grin appeared. "Let's go home then and I'll do whatever you want."

"Whatever?" I sat at the edge of the counter now, half my arse on it, half not.

He nodded once.

I could feel my cheeks flush, but we'd already had sex. Several times. So I should be able to talk about it and communicate what I wanted. "And if I said I wanted you stretched out on the bed, unmoving, as I did whatever *I* wanted to *you*?"

His eyes, already dark naturally, got even darker. "I'm down with that too."

I just bet he was. Still, I didn't think he'd let me do all the work on my own... but as long as I got to map out his body, properly study his tattoos, and suck his dick... then he could do whatever he wanted to me afterwards.

CHAPTER 8

"*S*o what did you want to talk to me about?" Adam asked the next day, as soon as we sat down at a table with our lunch.

I had a sandwich, he'd gone for pasta salad. "It wasn't that serious, really. It's fixed now." I'd gone back and forth with myself whether I should tell him or not. Wynn had helped me move out of Al's flat, and it was all over with him now, so… why tell Adam when I was done?

What he didn't know wouldn't hurt him. If I told him the truth about Al now, he'd end up angry on my behalf. That would sure be nice, but it wouldn't serve any purpose.

I was done with Al. Hopefully he'd let me be from now on, though I couldn't quite hold out hope he'd let me end it on my terms just yet. I hadn't heard from him, anyway, so that was good.

"It seemed pretty serious to me." And of course Adam wasn't going to simply let it go. "And you said you'd tell me all about it, remember? Don't go backing out now."

I had said that. "I just needed to ask your help. And if I could stay with you and Nick for a while. But it's okay now, really, no need for it."

"Stay with Nik and me?" He blinked, then grimaced. "I don't think that would've been possible anyway. We're not... I mean, like, we're not in a good place right now."

They weren't? "What happened?" Adam had sounded happy on the phone yesterday. I'd assumed he'd had a great time with Nick—likely shagging—as I knew they didn't get to spend much time together anymore with their schedules.

"Ahh..." He fidgeted a little on his chair. "Well, you know, I kinda—no, not kinda, I *did*... cheat on him."

My eyes widened in surprise. "You cheated on Nick? Why?" They'd always been so tight. They'd got together during college and had stayed together, all open and committed to each other.

He dragged a hand through his hair. "Because I wanted to? Basically, I've figured out I'm not made out to be what he wants."

"What do you mean?" Adam had always been happy with Nick… hadn't he?

"Happy ever afters are fucking boring, is what." He leant back in his chair, staring briefly up at the ceiling. "I'm young. I've barely started my twenties. I want to live my life a little, not settle down. I want to fuck whoever I want; I want to have *fun*. And Nick… he's not into that. He wants stability and monogamy and all that shit and I just… I thought I wanted it, you know? A relationship like the one my brother has, but I don't." He sighed heavily.

Now this was a new side to Adam. I knew he liked to party, but that he'd give up his relationship for it… that I hadn't realised.

"I've been hanging out with Cooper a lot," he said then. "First time I cheated on Nick was with him."

Cooper? Bloody hell. But of course it had to be.

"And after that it just kinda continued, you know? With Cooper, other guys, girls—"

"Girls?" I exclaimed, shocked.

He grimaced. "Why does everyone presume I'm gay just because I've been with Nick since I was sixteen? I'm not, you know."

"You've never said…"

"Yeah, well." He continued dragging a hand through his blond hair, messing up the styled spikes. "It's never come up, has it? And it's never really mattered because of Nick. But there you have it. I go either way when it comes to sex. As for relationships... I think I prefer guys there, but you never know."

I couldn't believe all this had been going on with Adam and I hadn't noticed.

"So you couldn't have stayed with me, because Nick and I aren't good. I'm using the guest room for now until we can figure out what to do with the flat and all. It's ours, so either we sell it or one of us buys the other out or... yeah, we've got to figure something out. Anyway, we're not together anymore and not really on speaking terms either at the moment."

Oh wow. Good thing I had come clean to Wynn then. And Wynn... not once had he blamed me for essentially lying to him. And I'd kind of cheated too, hadn't I? But Al wasn't nice like Nick, he didn't love me the way Nick loved Adam.

"So do you still need a place to stay?" he asked, steering the conversation away from himself and back to me. "Cooper's got a guest room, in case you need it. I don't think he'll mind. He likes you."

Likes me? "Umm, no, it's okay."

Adam grinned wickedly, bracing his forearms on the table and leaning forward a little. "No need to blush like that, Kaz. Sure, I don't think Cooper would've said no to a shag if you offered, but he generally thinks you're a good person. He worries about you almost as much as I do at work."

Why did everyone worry about me at work? Was it really that obvious that I wasn't comfortable, that I didn't like it, that I couldn't *do* it? That I wasn't cut out to be a bartender? "I haven't really spoken much to Cooper." He tended to stay behind the bar all night, not taking many breaks. Whenever he did, he was busy flirting with people—or Adam. Now I thought about it, maybe Adam had flirted back a lot too, but since he'd been with Nick I'd never given it any serious thought.

"Cooper's a decent lad, so if you still need a place to crash, I'll ring him up right now."

"Oh, no, it's fine now, really." Adam had been honest with me. I should return that favour and be honest with him too. "I broke up with Al."

His brows drew together in a frown. "You did? Why? *When?*"

"Well, yesterday, basically." I swallowed, thinking back to the note I'd left. He must've been furious when he came home and found it, but he hadn't called or texted me. Not yet, anyway.

"I'm sorry?" he offered quietly, obviously trying to read me.

"Don't be," I murmured. "It's been a long time coming. I just… I had to find a place to go before I could end it, because I could never live with him after that. He wouldn't have let me end it if I continued to live with him." Then he would've probably forced me to sex too, which he'd never actually done before. Guilt-tripped me into sucking his dick, maybe, but never outright force.

"What do you mean?" The frown from before was back, deeper now. "He wouldn't have *let* you?"

"It means exactly that." I licked my upper lip, then nibbled nervously on the bottom one. "You can't tell anyone, Adam, but... he's not a nice person. I know he seems like it from the outside, but he's really not. He's never left a bruise anywhere visible, but—he likes to slap me around." And slapping my face didn't usually leave bruises as compared to when he used his fists. Not that that was often, but even once was enough.

"The fuck?" And like that, Adam's calm, happy demeanour was gone. "That fucker's hurt you?" His hands fisted.

It warmed to know he cared about me. "It's over now, okay?" I didn't want him to do anything on my behalf. As long as Al stayed away, I was happy to let him be.

"I swear I'll hurt *him*," Adam murmured, clenching and unclenching his fists. "You don't hit people who doesn't deserve it. If I so much as see him touch you, I swear I'll hit him in the face. And I hit hard."

A startled chuckle left me. "Wynn said something like that too."

He froze, eyes widening a fraction. "Wynn?"

Oh! Well… Shit.

"As in… *Wynn?*" Adam's anger bled away to be replaced by surprise, eagerness, and then he seemed like he couldn't quite believe the conclusion he'd come to. "You're shagging Wynn?" He dragged both hands over his face, laughing. "Wow. I've seen many people try to get him on the hook when he's out and about in the club, but no one's ever succeeded. Cooper said Wynn rejected him too once. How'd you manage to seduce him?"

"It wasn't so much seduction," I mumbled, partly embarrassed and partly pleased by the fact Wynn didn't seem to get with everyone who threw themselves at his feet. "The day I botched my audition, when you left after work… He found me bawling my eyes out. I don't think there was anything sexy at all about that situation."

He turned thoughtful. "Three days ago? That's when you first met?"

I nodded. "I went home with him. Not for… you know… but because I was a wreck and I couldn't go back home to Al's like that. But Wynn didn't mind. He comforted me. He was so nice. No one's ever been that nice to me."

Adam's frown was back. "Then you haven't met many nice people, Kaz."

"He said the same thing," I chuckled darkly. "And I guess not. Besides my family, there's only you and Mathilda. Al's never really cared, and I was stupid to think he did. I should've realised it before I moved in with him, but... I guess I fancied him too much and was just happy that he fancied me back."

"I never noticed anything amiss," he said then. "I mean, I'd noticed you sneaking off together. And when you moved in together, I thought it was rather obvious. Then again, I couldn't fathom living with someone I wasn't sleeping with." He grinned wryly. "So now you're living with Wynn, huh?"

"Yeah." Wynn was at home. He'd said he'd do some work while I was out. "Four days in and I'm living with him... It sounds mental, I know. But... I don't want Kian to find out what Al's like. It wouldn't do him any good to find out the guy he really likes doesn't treat me well."

"Why not?" Adam asked. "I mean, he should know what a twat Alistair is, shouldn't he? He can't go around liking a guy who's been hitting his little brother. I don't care how charming and nice he is to everyone else—as long as he's hurt you, he's fucking dead to me."

My chest squeezed tight. "What if he doesn't believe me, though?"

"Oh, come on, now don't you be a twat." Adam rolled his eyes. "Of course Kian will believe you. You're his brother, for God's sake. Why would you lie about something like that, anyway?"

"I reckon lots of people do," I mumbled, uncomfortable now. "For attention or… something."

"Not lots of people. A select few, perhaps. But you wouldn't." He stared hard at me. "You should've told me before. Hell, you should've told me everything after the first time he hit you. I would've taken care of him."

Adam was all buff and muscular like Wynn. He had tattoos and piercings to match too—at least the piercings in his ears, I'd never heard Adam mention he had pierced anything else. But where Wynn was all dark and intense and mysterious, Adam was fair and optimistic and a more happy-go-lucky sort of guy.

"I'm sorry." I bowed my head. "I know… but—I don't know. I guess in the end he made me think I deserved it? But I'm tired of being someone's dirty secret. He didn't even want to look at me during— well, you know—" I couldn't explicitly say *sex*, there were too many people around us who might pick up on that words. "It was always just me getting him off, never the other way around."

Adam's expression was sour. "I never would've thought he'd treat someone like that. That fucking hypocrite. What's he so damn afraid or ashamed of anyway? Mathilda's brother and nephew are gay, I'm in a gay relationship... Did he think people would mind? Instead he acted all straight while secretly keeping you on the side? And as if that's not bad enough, he's not even nice to you and he doesn't give you what you deserve, in or out of bed."

Adam's a good friend. I smiled at him, but I could feel my face was flushed. "Can we forget about Al? I'm done with him... I don't want him to cloud my life now. Wynn, he's—well, it's only been four days, but he's good to me."

A wicked gleam appeared in Adam's eyes, the sour mood from before gone in the blink of an eye. He was easy like that, Adam; it wasn't often he was in a bad mood, and when it was it never lasted long. "So, tell me, Kaz... How is Wynn in bed?"

I should've known this was coming. "I'm not telling you that."

He laughed. "Just tell me one thing?"

I nodded, but it was a bit reluctant.

"Is he good to you? Both in *and* out of bed?"

I flushed a deeper shade of red, but this was a question that was easy to answer. One I could answer without dying of embarrassment, because Adam only asked it out of worry for me. "Yeah. He is." *Very much so.*

"Good." Adam sat back in his chair. "Because if he isn't, I will personally kick his arse, and I don't give a fuck about my job, if it comes to it."

That startled a laugh out of me. "Don't worry. I don't think you have to worry about losing your job anytime soon." Wynn might look tough—and maybe he was to others—but not to me. He made me feel special. He *was* special.

And fuck it all, but all I wanted was to go back home to him.

Maybe Adam saw it, because he grinned. "You in a hurry?"

"No," I said hurriedly. Wynn was busy with work, after all. He'd said he had a lot to do, to take my time. So I shouldn't come home an hour after I'd left and interrupt him. "Not in a hurry at all."

He snorted. "I remember what it was like way back when I first got with Nick. I couldn't wait to see him again if we were apart for even a minute. All I wanted to do, all day long, was to rip his clothes off and have fun."

That wasn't quite what I'd had in mind, but then again... I wouldn't *mind* would I? Sex with Wynn was addictive—and I was already an addict.

CHAPTER 9

*W*ynn was stretched out on the sofa when I came back. "I cleaned out some shelves for you in the bedroom," he said, waving that way while keeping his focus on the TV. He said it almost nonchalantly, like it wasn't a big deal…

But when I entered the bedroom, I saw that he hadn't just cleaned out *some* space. Almost half the wardrobe was empty, waiting for my clothes that were still packed into suitcases and stacked in the hall.

My chest squeezed, a lump stuck in my throat, and I fought against my entirely too emotional self. *He's cleaned out space for me—because he actually wants me to stay here.* I'd thought it was a done deal, but now, with all these emotions flooding me, I knew I hadn't been fully convinced. But I was now.

I walked back into the living room and around the sofa, to stand over him. He looked up at me slowly, almost warily. "What?"

"Thank you." I sank down on my knees and bent forward to hug him. "I don't know what I would've done without you right now." I'd very likely still be living with Alistair if it wasn't for him. I didn't even want to think about that, though, so I turned my head, seeking his lips.

He didn't say anything, but he answered me with his kiss. It was hard and desperate and soft all at the same time and I fell into it, leaning over him, one hand slowly running down over his chest, stomach, and finally over his crotch.

His hips bucked, giving me a handful of what hid underneath the jeans. *I want to make him feel good. The way he makes me feel.* So I pulled away from the kiss and shuffled over so I was leaning over his crotch instead.

"Kasey?" He propped up on his elbows to look down at me.

"*Shh,*" was all I said as I unzipped his jeans and tugged lightly at them so they were pulled down to just under his arse. His dick was half-hard, poking slightly out of the boxers that had been tugged down too.

I licked a line from his balls to the tip.

"Ahh, fuck." He fell back down, hips and neck arching. "*Yeah.*"

I teased the piercings with my tongue, licked the whole length some more, sucked on the tip… and then finally took him into my mouth properly. He wasn't fully hard yet, but he'd soon get there.

As I stared bobbing my head, his hands tangled in my hair—not to the point it hurt or to where he was guiding me, just gently resting there, almost massaging my scalp.

I pulled off him and moved down to give some attention to his balls, sucking first one into my mouth, then the other. I rolled them in my hand, squeezing gently, then licked up his already hard and spit-slick dick. *I really like sucking cock.* Especially like this, with someone I knew wouldn't just leave me high and dry after. I could continue this all day, if it wasn't so damn good. His pre-come was salty and *mmm*, I just loved the taste of it on my tongue.

"Want to come?" I asked, wrapping my hand around his length to stroke.

"Yeah," he answered, voice strained, a little breath-less. His eyes were closed, his hips bucking slightly into my hand.

I'd halfway hoped he'd say he'd rather fuck me, but this was good too. I could suck him to completion and get a mouthful of come at the same time. And it didn't take long, because he was already close. A couple deep-throats, some more sucking combined with stroking him, and semen splattered in my mouth.

I sucked the tip greedily as I swallowed what he gave me.

"Fuck. Kasey." He let his fingers untangle from my hair, arms sliding down to grab at my arms and haul me up for a lazy kiss. I stretched out on top of him, cupping his neck and the side of his face as our lips slid together.

Now this I could do all day too. Just lying on him like this, sharing kisses that ranged from closed-lipped chaste ones to tongue-diving deep ones. I was so in lust with this man I'd gladly give up everything just to stay in bed with him. We wouldn't even need food... for a while anyway.

"How about you fuck my mouth today?" he said eventually, when he'd come down from his own orgasm.

My breath hitched. I *liked* that idea. "Yeah?" I asked hopefully.

"Yeah." And he sounded so *sure* and this was exciting, because this was something I'd never done before. No one had ever let me do this to them, it was always the other way around.

I rose up on my knees, unzipped my jeans and pulled them and my briefs down. My cock was already hard, slapping against my lower stomach as it was freed from its tight confines.

Wynn watched it with a small smile, then shot a quick look up at me.

I scooted forwards until my dick was within reach of his mouth. The tip tapped gently against his lips and Wynn parted them, letting me in. He bobbed up on down a few times, sucking me, slicking me up with spit. Then he simply lay back, parted his lips and left the job to me.

I braced my arms over his head, at the arm of the sofa and started thrusting, slowly at first, not sure how fast or deep I could go. But when he grabbed my arse and pushed me into going faster, I gladly went with it. His gag reflex seemed to be non-existent, because I could bury my dick to the root without him giving any protest. I wasn't as big as him, but still, having a cock nudge the back of your throat was bound to trigger it if it was there at all.

His hands kneaded my arse cheeks, finger sliding down my arse to rub against my hole.

"*Oh!*" I faltered as the finger, slick with spit, pressed into me, but then I started again with new vigour. I was *so close*—

He didn't swallow, as his jaw was still loose so I could fuck his mouth through my orgasm. And I did, gladly so, not stopping until I had nothing more to give. I slumped over him, resting my forehead on the back of my hands. My dick had started to soften and I pulled my hips back from his face.

He chuckled deep in his throat. "Fuck, Kasey, that was—" He wiped come and spit off his chin, licking it off his hand so he wouldn't make a mess of it.

"You're really neat, aren't you?" It slipped out on a laugh as I stared down at him.

He rolled his eyes back to look at me. "I hate clutter. And messes. I've lived in shitholes when I was a kid— I'm not living like that now."

So there was a reason to his almost-OCD cleanliness. I scooted backwards so I could rest fully on top of him again, tucking my head in the crook of his neck. "Is that why you cleaned out space for me? To get rid of my stuff?"

"Partly," he admitted. "But I also want you to know you're welcome here."

My heart did a funny little flutter. "I already know that." But showing it like he'd just done... I appreciated more than I could explain in words. "Want to help me unpack?"

So that's what we finally dragged ourselves off the

sofa to do. We took a suitcase each into the bedroom and flipped them open almost at the same time. I put away socks and T-shirts and underwear, whereas he'd opened the one where my clothes were wrapped around some of my DVD collection.

"What's this?" He held one of the DVDs up. "You watch cartoons?"

"That is not cartoons," I huffed, offended. "It's *anime*."

He gave me an unimpressed stare. "It's cartoons."

I walked over and took the DVD from him. "Anime is not cartoons. They're totally different. Anime is a piece of art. It differs from other forms of animation by styles, methods, production, and in process."

He sighed heavily. "It's cartoons for kids."

"It is not—" Had he never watched anime before? Didn't he know how amazing it was compared to crappy cartoons I'd used to watch before I discovered there was something better out there?

"It's *about* kids." He pointed at the cover.

I stared down at it, and yes, the main characters were kids, but... "They grow up. And they save the world and shit. Except it's a lot more complicated than that and I can't really explain it without you watching some for yourself—but anyway, it's awesome. Have you *never* watched anime? Seriously? Not even *hentai*?"

His expression didn't change.

Now I was the one to sigh. "Well, *hentai* is basically porn. Animated porn."

"I don't like porn much." He grimaced slightly.

My eyes might as well bug out of their sockets. "You don't like *porn*? But—" All the things we'd done in the few days we'd been together... that was pretty porn-y. How could he not like to watch porn? Oh, the things I was learning about him.

"I'd rather read a good book, honestly." He took more DVDs out of my suitcase—all of them anime. He studied the covers, glanced at the blurbs on the back of them, and threw them on the bed. "So you're really into this shit?"

"It's not shit." I was going to show him. "How about you watch some with me? My favourites. I swear, you'll like it." Except I couldn't make such a promise could I? It wasn't like I actually knew him yet. I had no idea if he'd like the same things I did or not.

"We'll see." He glanced at me. "Footloose and cartoons, huh? What's next?"

I frowned. How did he know I liked Footloose?

"You watched it on my Netflix, remember?" He reminded me, grinning as he straightened up. "Dance flicks and Japanese animation. What else is there to know about you?"

"Nothing. I think." That was pretty much it. "Umm… well, I like to read fan fiction."

"Fan fiction?" His eyebrows inched up his forehead.

"Yeah, fan fiction of the shows I watch. You know, when things don't happen the way you want them to or you ship a couple that's not actually canon, and… well, yeah, fan fiction is great for that. Also, most of the fan fiction I read are pretty sexual as it's usually a ship between two guys. You can get lots of ideas from it really." Not that I'd ever lived out any fantasies I might've had, or got from reading, but with Wynn I might just get to do it. "Then again, if you don't like to watch porn, and only like to read *good books*, then I'm sure you don't like to read erotica either."

He snorted. "I've got space in the DVD racks in the living room for these." He pointed at the covers on the bed.

"Oh, I've got more than these," I warned, noticing how he easily ignored my observation. "A *lot* more. Not all of it anime though. I've got some films—I especially like superhero films, like Marvel—and series."

"Now Marvel I could get behind," he said, grinning like he was pleased he'd found some middle ground. "Action flicks in general."

I liked superhero action, but if he liked other sort of action—explosions and car chases and whatnot—then I was out. Though action in a fantasy setting, like The Lord of the Rings, *that* I could do.

"We should have a film marathon one night we're not working," I suggested lightly, smiling down at my DVDs. I only bought the series I liked, after all, so they were all precious to me. Al had never been fond of them though, so if I'd watched it back at his place, it had mostly been in my room, on my laptop.

A strong arm slid around my neck, drawing me back against a wide, hard chest. Soft lips brushed my temple. "Now that we could do."

I closed my eyes briefly as I leaned back against him. He stayed like that too, his cheek resting against my head, arm still around me in a loose hug.

"I like learning new things about you," he said then, voice low and deep.

"Same here." I smiled to myself. "And there's a lot more to learn. That's a bit exciting, isn't it?" I knew the most fundamental though—how kind he was and how considerate of me, both in and out of bed. That he liked keeping his place clean and tidy. That no matter what people said about him, he had a big heart. Nothing anyone else said could make me see him any differently—because what mattered was how he treated me, and he treated me better than anyone had ever done.

He was like a knight in shining armour—the modern type, who was all dark and brooding and not shiny at all, but a saviour anyway. He'd protect me. He wouldn't let anything bad happen to me as long as he was around. And he probably would be around for a while as we figured out this strange, new relationship we'd fallen into.

I couldn't be anything but happy at that.

CHAPTER 10

$\mathcal{L}$ ife seemed a lot easier. Maybe because I didn't live in fear in my own home anymore, maybe because I'd had a good shift at work last night where I didn't mess up much, or maybe just because all the sex I had now left me constantly relaxed and in a good mood?

All of them might certainly be helping. As for work doing better... if it was because of Wynn's help or because I wasn't constantly worried about Al... the jury was still out on that one. Being more relaxed—and not a bundle of nerves, like Wynn said—certainly helped too.

So here I was, at my brother's place to have a Friday dinner with them. I had today off, but would work again tomorrow. It seemed a little easier to face the bar when I had a night off in-between shifts. I hoped tomorrow would happen without me messing up too much either.

"There you are!" Kian drew me into a tight hug the minute I stepped through the door.

"It's not been that long." I chuckled and tried to save my dignity by fighting my way out of his grip. It didn't work—even Kian was stronger than me. We weren't anything alike, not really, but then I got most of my mum's Asian genes and Kian's mum was Caucasian... but we were both femme. Kian currently had his black hair dyed with rainbow tips, which he seemed to do at least once a year. Eyeliner marked his eyes. He wore a tight T-shirt without any print, but it was a pastel pink so it relayed its message anyway. And standard skinny jeans—exactly like mine.

While my hair was its regular coarse black, I also wore eyeliner. I'd used to dye my hair before too—back in school I'd had a period while it'd been pink. Then Al had happened and he certainly hadn't liked *that*, so I'd coloured it over with black again after a while. Alistair didn't like anything that made me look camp.

"I'm worried about you, you idiot." He held me at arms' length and looked me up and down. "How're you doing? Al's been by several times in the past week.

He's real worried about you, says you haven't been home and he's not been able to get a hold of you."

I swear my blood froze. "Al's been here?"

"Yeah, looking for *you*." He tilted his head. "What's going on?"

I swallowed. "We broke up. That's to say—I broke up with him. I moved out." And I'd left the note... Hadn't he got the hint? How could he come around to my brother's and claim to look for me, claim I still lived with him? And he *hadn't* tried to contact me—not after I'd moved all my stuff out anyway.

Kian blinked. "You moved out? But... where are you living now?"

I mumbled the address, but didn't mention I lived with anyone in particular. I didn't think Kian knew Wynn's address anyway. Best to let Kian get used to me and Al being over first before I brought Wynn into the mix. I did not want to hear how surely Al was the better catch because he so wasn't.

"So if Al comes here asking for me again, don't tell him anything." I gave him a pleading look now, and when I spotted movement at the corner of my eye, I turned to give Silver one as well. "It's over. I don't want to keep seeing him."

Silver's eyes narrowed slightly, but he nodded. Kian, on the other hand, frowned. "But you've been in love with him for years. What changed?"

I shrugged. I didn't want to get into it. Kian would flip his shit and I was *fine* now. As long as Al stayed away, anyway. Which he probably wouldn't do, but I wouldn't worry about it until I had to. "Sometimes people just fall out of love, I guess." Especially when they get slapped around and belittled all the time.

Now that was something Kian didn't want to believe either. He'd been with Silver for years now and he was a hardcore romantic, so the possibility of falling out of love didn't sit well with him. Still, it made him shut up, grimace, and turn to the kitchen. "So I tried to cook dinner for once, but failed majorly, so we ordered take-away from the Indian place down the street. Hope that's okay?"

Way to liven the mood, brother. I chuckled as I followed him, brushing past Silver still leaning against the doorway. "That's good. I've never had much confidence in your cooking abilities anyway." He was as bad at cooking as I was. Sure, we could do noodles and pop things into the microwave or a pizza in the oven, but preparing actual meals... that wasn't our forte. Better to go the safe route of take-away.

"Want to see a film while we eat?" Kian asked, eyeing me wryly as we piled food on our plates. "We can go for a romantic comedy, maybe? For laughs, you know? Or if you're entirely done with romance, I suppose we could do action? Or if you're *really, really* done with romance, horror? Nothing says fuck you like some blood and gore."

I couldn't help but laugh at that. "I'd be good with whatever you two want to watch." I glanced at Silver, who still hadn't said a word, to find he was already watching me. I flushed and looked back at my plate, ladling tikka masala over the rice I'd already piled on.

When I was younger, back when Kian had first met Silver and brought him over to meet the family, I'd fancied him *so* bad. He'd been the first boy, the first person, I'd ever fancied. It was because of him I'd figured out I was gay. Looking at him now, there were some similarities to Wynn. Like the black hair and the fit body and the full sleeve tattoos.

I didn't fancy Silver anymore though. I'd grown out of it right around the time I'd started to fancy Alistair instead. Now it was Wynn who occupied my thoughts. That made three guys in the span of five or six years? That wasn't so bad.

Mathilda had fancied countless guys during our two years at college. Some she'd got with, some she hadn't. Me? Well, there'd only been Al through those two years. I'd never once looked at anyone else— though I *had* sucked other guys' dicks. I'd just never fancied them.

And now Wynn...

"You seem deep in thought." Silver bumped my shoulder with his gently. "You sure you're all right?"

"Yeah." I smiled to convince him, but I wasn't sure he was convinced. He only gave me another long once-over, then grabbed cutlery and a glass and took his plate with him out to the living room.

I followed. I let them sit together on one end of the sofa and took the other, curling up with my plate on the armrest.

Silver browsed through channels, didn't find anything, and Kian popped a DVD into the player. He'd chosen an action comedy, probably to be on the safe side. Truth was though, I wouldn't have minded a romantic comedy. I was in a pretty good place right now, but I wasn't ready to tell him that. Wasn't ready to hear about how Al was better than Wynn. I didn't even know why he didn't like Wynn, as I'd never paid much attention.

The film didn't hold my attention. I kept cutting glances their way. They'd been together for so many years now and they were comfortable together. They always had been, honestly. When Kian brought Silver home for Christmas their first year together... he'd been so happy.

I'd overheard Mum and Dad saying later, after they'd gone home again, that they'd never seen Kian so happy before. Not in the few months he'd been in our lives by then, anyway. I hadn't grown up with my brother, as he'd been living with his no-good mum. But when he turned eighteen and Dad could finally contact him again without her making a mess of it… Kian had entered my life and he'd a fixed part of it ever since.

I loved him. And I loved Silver, he was almost like an older brother to me now too. He spent more time with our family than his own, after all, and with all those years together… yeah, they were solid.

That was what I wanted. Something solid, someone to feel comfortable with, someone to love fully. It was what Kian and Silver had, it was what Adam had used to have with Nick. Except Adam wasn't interested in this anymore in favour of sleeping around. But I was. I didn't want to sleep around. All I'd ever wanted was someone to love, someone who was only mine.

It seemed like maybe, possibly, that's what Wynn wanted too. Why else would we have moved so quickly in such a short amount of time? Surely not just for the sex. It was great, but there was more to it than that.

Two phones *pinged* at the same time. One was mine —the other Kian's. I shuffled the last forkful of food into my mouth before I checked what was going on.

I almost choked on my food. It was a text message. From Al.

Where the fuck are you, Kaz?

Next second, another one trickled in.

Don't you dare avoid me. I have to see you.

I managed to swallow the food before I really did choke, but only barely and I didn't taste it at all.

"Is it okay if Chloe stops by?" I heard Kian ask, but it was almost like I heard it coming from very far away, like he was in a different room.

I'm warning you, Kaz.

That one had an angry emoji after it and I stared at the red, angry face. That was probably how he looked right now too. Why he'd spent so many days in silence before he contacted me was beyond me, but... my peace was over. Maybe he'd hoped I'd come back on my own? As if that would ever happen.

"She'll be here any second," Kian was saying, still as if far away. "She was just around the corner."

You can't fucking ignore me, you piece of shit, you hear that?

So what if he found me? I was surrounded by people. Right now I was with Kian and Silver, and they wouldn't let Al hurt me. If I wasn't with them, I was with Wynn, and at work I was around Adam, mostly. Neither of them would let Al hurt me either—and considering both of them knew he *would*, they wouldn't let him near me.

It was weird that Al had resorted to threatening messages. He'd never done that before. He was always nice and cordial in public or anywhere else someone other than me could get a hold of. These text messages… They could be used as evidence to show people, like Kian, what he was really like.

Should I show him? I clenched my new phone tight, glanced at him, seeing him smile adoringly up at Silver who affectionally ruffled his hair. Kian's expression changed to one of indignation as he pushed at Silver's chest—not managing to so much as move him an inch, but he did retract his hand. Kian instantly set to fixing his hair just so again.

The door slammed open and Chloe stormed in before I could make up my mind. She wore high heels that she toed off angrily before she came over to flop onto the sofa, in-between Kian and me. She was dressed up as if she'd been to a party, but her expression was thunderous and her eyeliner and mascara were slightly smudged under her eyes. Eyes that were a bit glassy, as if she had been crying or she would soon.

"I hate everyone," she pronounced.

"Aww, babe." Kian looped his arms around her neck and hugged her tight. "Don't put us all under there just because one guy's an arsehole."

She blew out a breath. "I try and try and try. And this is all I get! Dumped. And only a month before Christmas too. I don't know why I bother."

I let my hands sink to my lap, still clutching my phone tight. I couldn't show Kian now. He had other things to occupy him, like his best friend clearly being dumped.

When I'd first met Chloe, she'd been in a relationship with another girl. A tomboyish girl, but still a girl. She'd been the first lesbian I'd ever known back then, while Kian had been the first gay guy. But it had turned out Chloe *wasn't* a lesbian. When that relationship ended, her next one had been with a guy. And so she had continued through the years, switching between girls and guys at her leisure.

She seemed to want to find the right girl or guy for her, but she never managed. Her relationships never lasted wrong. Either she was really difficult to deal with—hard to imagine, as she'd always been really nice to me—or she fell for the wrong type of people. It was probably the latter.

"I suppose it's good it's before Christmas though." She sighed. "At least I hadn't got around to buying him a Christmas gift yet."

"See? There's a silver lining to everything," Kian quipped, always the optimist. "You and Kaz can start a club. He's newly single too."

Oh! Shit.

Chloe turned her head to me. "Yeah? I bet your ex is an arsehole too."

If only any of you knew. I tried for a smile but it turned out rather weak. "Yeah."

Kian's brows knitted together in a frown as he watched me, while Silver only gave me another long look like he had in the kitchen earlier. *Does he suspect something?* Kian sure didn't, but it was harder to read Silver.

"Men," Chloe huffed. "Next time it's going to be a woman, for sure."

"As if some of them aren't only after sex too," Kian commented drily.

Chloe sighed, as if he had a point. "Maybe I'll try being a nun for a while. Celibacy's got to have some perks right?"

"If not you can always go for a dildo," Kian offered kindly. "You get the dick but without all the drama that comes with the rest of the body."

Silver hit Kian upside the head—and Chloe burst out laughing. "Thanks a lot for that," Silver grumbled.

"Not you." Kian turned wide eyes on him. Wide eyes that always made Silver melt. I'd seen it myself countless times. "Never you. If anything, I'm the one who makes the drama in our relationship."

Silver wrapped an arm around Kian's neck and drew him in close. "That's right."

I smiled a little to myself at their antics, but as I glanced down at my phone and saw Al's messages still on the screen, my smile faded. I wanted to go back to Wynn's flat and be with him, let him make it all better, because he would. When I was with him, nothing else mattered. Al couldn't get to me, *no one* could, because I was safe with Wynn.

"Guys, I'm going home." I stood abruptly, shutting off the screen on my phone so I didn't have to look at Al's threatening messages anymore.

"What?" Kian pushed away from Silver. "Why? You just got here a little while ago."

I bit down on my lip. "I'm not feeling so great. Need some time alone." *Some quality time in bed with Wynn,* was more like it, but I wasn't going to say that.

"Ahh, yeah, I'm sorry." Kian got to his feet and came over to hug me again. "About the audition and Al and everything. You've not had a good week, have you?"

I hugged him back. "Yeah, no, not really." The audition… I tried not to think about that. That I had to wait a year to retake it and then another one to even start school *if* I did get in. But other than that… getting away from Al only meant good things, and Wynn… yeah, I didn't have words to explain Wynn. "I'm working tomorrow night. Got Sunday off, but, yeah, we'll just talk next week, okay?" Sunday I planned on spending with Wynn. All day, uninterrupted.

"Okay. Don't feel too down, you hear me? It's not

the end of the world that you botched that audition…
and when it comes to boyfriends, there's plenty other
fish in the sea."

I chuckled. "Yeah, there is." One in particular was
likely waiting for me at home.

CHAPTER 11

"*H*ey, Wynn..." I walked into his office without knocking since there were only the two of us in the club yet and the door wasn't even closed properly.

He put something down quickly and sat up, staring at me.

I stopped, blinking. "What was that?"

"Nothing." But his hand couldn't hide the paperback it was splayed over. Nor could it hide the picture of two naked chests on the cover.

My nervousness from before was instantly replaced by a startled laugh and I walked over until I stood against his desk. "Are you reading gay romance novels?"

"No." But he didn't quite look at me as he said that.

"You are." I swatted his hand away and took the book from him. He only half-heartedly tried to take it back. It *was* a picture of two naked male torsos over a landscape on the cover. I opened the book to a random page, skimmed some words, and quickly found out I was in the middle of a sex scene. "I thought you said you didn't like porn."

"It's not porn." But he still wouldn't look at me.

I read further down the page. "Not porn? Really? What's this then? *'He wrapped his hand around the erect cock and guided it to—'*"

"Okay, okay!" He snapped the book back and dropped it into a drawer. I swear he was the one flushing now, and *that* was something I hadn't seen yet in the six days I'd been with him.

This was *hilarious.* "You're reading porn novels and yet you get on *my* case for watching anime? Do I have to remind you which is the most perverted out of those two?"

He glowered up at me. "It's not porn."

"Seemed like it to me. It explained in detail exactly how they had some hot, heavy, raw butt sex." I wasn't a stranger to reading sex scenes, but the ones I read were usually in all the fan fiction I consumed when I was obsessed with a series and the characters in it.

"Yeah, yeah, keep teasing and see just how much

sex you're gonna get in the future," he muttered mutinously.

It startled a laugh out of me, because that was almost... petulant. "Are you threatening to withhold sex?" I walked around the desk to stand next to him.

He swivelled his chair around so he faced me, wry grin back in place. "Would it work?"

It so definitely would. "I don't know. Maybe. Try and find out."

"Nah, I really can't be arsed." He slung an arm around my waist and pulled me onto his lap. I almost overbalanced, but his arm was strong, and I grabbed onto his shoulders, so I managed to stay seated.

"Shouldn't you be working instead of reading?" I looped my arms around his neck and moved to straddle him instead of sitting with both my feet to one side.

"I'm done. Did you get some practice in? I figured I wouldn't watch you today so you didn't have to go all clumsy on me again." His hands slipped down my side, thumbs brushing under the hem of my shirt to find bare skin.

"I did. But I'm done too." I'd taken advantage of the empty club and all the floor space, but there was only so much practice I could get in knowing that it wouldn't be long till the club opened and my co-workers would be in soon.

"Oh yeah?" he murmured, lips brushing over my jaw. "Then what on earth are we going to do until it's time to open?"

"I've got some ideas." Mainly, I wanted to get on my knees and suck his dick. I couldn't get enough of it. And the piercings still fascinated me to no end. I pressed the palm of my hand against his cock to get my message even more pointedly across.

He huffed, then grabbed my arse, surged out of the chair and turned around to deposit me in it. "Ahh!" I sprawled in it, surprised and not quite sure what was going on. Until he got on his knees in front of me anyway, spreading *my* knees, and I gained a clue. "Hey, I wanted to—"

"Yeah, I know." But he wouldn't let me, as evident from the fact he was already unzipping me. "But today is my turn. Just sit back and enjoy, Kasey." He pulled my jeans and boxers down enough to free my dick, then set to work.

My head thudded back against the back of the chair. I was slumped so much in it I was in danger of simply sliding out, but I put one foot on the edge to properly brace me. The other I spread even more to give him space.

His head was buried in my lap, nose in my pubes, as he took my hardening dick in, sucking it nice and good from flaccid to half-hard.

"Wynn…" I trailed off as my gaze cut to the side, staring at his nice, big, wide desk. "Do you have any lube around?"

My dick popped out of his mouth with a wet *pop*. "As a matter of fact, I do. Why?"

"Condoms?"

"Mmhm." He stroked my length, sucking greedily on the tip, swallowing the pre-come all but leaking out of me.

"Your desk," I choked out, trying to ignore the way the tip of his tongue ran over my slit and then down to circle my head. "It's all wide and big and I could lie on it—" I'd never had penetrative sex anywhere but in a bed.

With Al, it always happened in my bed, and after he'd got off—with me on my stomach, head buried in a pillow—he left to resume his daily activities or to go back to his own bed. I'd sucked his cock everywhere around the flat, but sex itself… no, never anywhere else. And here we were, with that wide expanse of wood available and instead I was slumped in a desk chair.

My words registered with him, because he stopped, gaze flicking up to look at me. "You want me to fuck you on my desk?"

"Y-yeah." Was that too much? Wouldn't he like that? I bit my lip anxiously. "It's okay if you don't—"

He stood up, dark eyes staring down at me, effectively silencing me. "Get on the desk then."

I was out of the chair in the blink of an eye, while he bent down to the bottom drawer and pulled out a condom and a small tube of lube.

"You fuck people in your office often?" I asked, eying it.

He snorted. "Hardly. This'll be the first time, actually." He undid his own jeans, pulling them down enough for his hard dick to slip free. "I just always figured it's wise to be prepared. You never know, right? And it's paid off now."

That it has. I smiled as I turned my back on him, pushing my clothes down past my arse. Getting out of my clothes completely felt a little too kinky—this was our workplace after all and what if we were interrupted and had to get dressed in a hurry? So for this time, this would have to do.

He came up behind me, slick fingers instantly finding my arse, sliding down my crack to rub at my hole. I braced my hands against the desk, widening my stance as much as possible while restricted by my skinny jeans. Two of his fingers slid into me and I arched my back, moaning softly before I could stop myself.

"That's it." He pressed close, cheek resting against

mine as he finger-fucked me gently. "Let me hear how much you like it."

I wasn't going to get any louder, if that's what he thought. Not in his office, with the door open, the club opening in not too long and co-workers set to arrive any second.

He pulled his fingers out. "Maybe this'll make you louder." And they were replaced by the head of his dick butting against me.

Oh! That felt good, as it breached me, the whole length slowly sliding inside. *Is he making this a challenge?* I wondered absentmindedly, tilting my head back against his neck. *To see how much he can make me moan?* In that case he was so going to lose. Maybe I'd let him win at home, but here? No way. Even if Al hadn't forbidden me from sounds and the habit had stuck... I wouldn't go full-out vocal in his damn office.

He slid back, almost all the way, then thrust back in.

I pitched forward, catching myself against the desk before I headbutted it, and the moan that left me did so without my permission. *Dammit. He's winning that challenge anyway.* And he knew it, because when I chanced a quick glance over my shoulder, he was grinning as he watched himself fuck my arse.

I folded my hands on top of the desk and rested my forehead against them, moving my hips in time with his thrusts. He was gripping my hips, his snapping back and forth in quick succession, and damn it all, but his dick was poking against my prostate and it was all just too mu—

"*Ahhh!*" I came without so much as touching my own dick, splattering the drawers of his desk with sticky white semen. "*Oh!*" That was surprising. It had never happened to me before.

He leant forward, draping over my back, and chuckled in my ear. "That's a good boy." His hips still snapped back and forth, driving his cock into my body again and again and leaving me unable to speak or think or do anything but try my best to *breathe.*

When he came, he stayed on top of me, forehead resting against my neck, as he got his own breathing under control.

Clapping brought us both into the here and now rather forcefully, both our heads shooting up to stare at the doorway. *Oh shit, shit, shit!* We'd spent too long, someone had come in for work and seen me get fucked by the boss—but it wasn't a co-worker. Not one I knew about anyway.

"Get the fuck out, Chad!" Wynn snapped.

He only laughed. "Get out? Hell, I'd join in if you'd let me."

Who the hell is he? He was clearly someone Wynn was familiar with. Speaking of Wynn, he was still buried in my arse, and the redhead was leaning against the doorway, grinning wickedly.

Wynn straightened, reached down to hold onto the condom as he pulled out, then hurried to be rid of it and pull his clothes up. All this he did while hiding his lower body behind me—and once he was done, I quickly pulled up my own underwear and skinny jeans before the redhead could get an eyeful.

"So you're getting kinky in your office now, huh?" he said, still leaning against the doorway, not making a move to come further into the room. "I thought you were a bit of a prude when it came to sex? You got that desperate?"

My face was red. I could feel it burn.

"Shouldn't you be in hospital?" Wynn grumbled, effectively ignoring the question. He zipped his jeans up, then grabbed some napkins he had on his desk to dry off his slick hand. The lube lay discarded on the desk, in plain sight, and I flushed even redder.

How much did he see? I hadn't given a thought to the door after Wynn slid into me. All that had existed in my world after that was Wynn—and his dick, fucking me so good I forgot anything else existed.

"I was discharged a few hours ago." He sighed, shuffling a little. "Back to scratch again. New drugs, new schedules. Let's hope it last longer than a couple years this time around."

Drugs? Was he sick?

Wynn put a hand on the small on my back, rubbing gently, but his focus remained on the redhead by the door. What had he said his name was again?

"Doesn't he work for you?" The redhead nodded to me, and when I dared look, I saw he was gazing at me appraisingly.

"He does," Wynn confirmed.

"Just be careful of a sexual harassment lawsuit, would you?" He blew out a breath. "You hear about those once in a while. It's never good."

I straightened instinctually. *Sexual harassment lawsuit?*

Wynn's hand left the small of my back and instead landed heavily across my shoulder, around my neck. "Mind your own business, Chad." *Right, that was his name.* "Besides, I doubt my own boyfriend's going to sue me."

My head turned so quickly I was afraid I'd suffer whiplash and my eyes widened. *He'd said the B-word.* It shouldn't come as a surprise, not really, considering I bloody lived with him... but he'd just admitted it out loud to *someone else*. He'd admitted to being my boyfriend to someone who was clearly his friend, and he'd done so almost... proudly. If I read him correct.

Chad's chuckled. "Boyfriend, huh? Wow. That's

great. And about damn time. It's been too long since Madison—"

"Chad," Wynn growled dangerously low, clearly a warning.

Madison. So that was the dead boyfriend. Didn't Wynn want to talk about him? Then again, he'd killed himself, so no matter how many years went by, that had to still hurt. They hadn't broken up, but his death had ended the relationship... It must've been really hard for Wynn to deal with.

"All right, all right." Chad held his hands up, palms out, in the universal sign for peace. "No talking about that. Gotcha."

I still had lube smeared in my arse and it was getting increasingly uncomfortable. "I'm gonna go get changed," I murmured to Wynn. It wasn't quite time to open the club yet, but I might as well get the bar ready.

He nodded, arm falling down to hang loosely at his side. I shuffled past him and over the floor—a walk that felt twice as long as it was with Chad staring at me.

"He's cute," I heard Chad say as I was out the door.

"What do you want?" Wynn growled, clearly not in a better mood even with me gone and the embarrassing situation he'd caught us out in behind us. "I'm busy. I've got work to do."

Considering I'd caught him reading a romance

novel, that wasn't exactly true. Or maybe he'd just taken a break—and then an even longer one as I came into the office? Maybe he actually was busy, but he'd taken enough time to spend some quality time fucking me? No matter what, I got a lot of a warmer welcome than Chad did. And he didn't grumble to me about being busy. In fact, he always made time for me, didn't he?

I couldn't help the wide smile spreading over my lips and I hurried over to the break room and my locker. I felt almost… giddy. And wasn't that a first?

CHAPTER 12

"*K*asey!" Wynn yelled from the edge of the bar.

Normally, yelling would've startled me, but the music was so loud that even yelling, his voice was almost drowned out.

"Uh oh," Cooper whispered as he slipped past me. "Sounds like someone's in trouble." But he gave me a teasing smile that made me instantly think that Adam had shared some juicy gossip with him.

I ambled over to Wynn. He was leaning against the bar, eyes only for me, and when I was opposite him, he leaned in so he wouldn't have to shout anymore. "If Chad comes to the bar, he's not allowed to buy anything."

"He gets free drinks?" I asked, just to be sure.

"No. He's not allowed to drink anything at all. Water, sure, alcohol? Never."

I blinked. "Uh, okay." I wanted to ask why, but didn't dare. The club was open and busy and people were packed, and what did it really matter anyway?

"He's mentally ill," Wynn said, leaning in further to speak against my ear. His stubbly cheek rasped against my smooth one. "Alcohol interferes with his meds and can induce mania."

Oh. Yes, that made sense. *Mania, huh?* Some forgotten memory came back, of listening to my brother speaking about this bloke who was bipolar. *Must've been Chad.* Or probably, anyway. He was the reason Kian knew Wynn, after all, had to be. Which meant he must be the friend Wynn had used to sleep with before his boyfriend died—and Chad shacked up with not just one but two lovers.

"He won't be getting any from me," I promised, and I hoped I would manage to keep that promise. I wasn't good at saying no. And standing my ground against someone wasn't my forte either. It was so much easier to simply back down.

"We'll be in my office. We've got some catching up to do." He ran his thumb over my lower lip and cheek quickly, then he was gone, retreating to the back of the club where only employees were allowed.

"Not that much trouble, eh?" Cooper waggled his eyebrows playfully.

"No." I rolled my eyes at him. "Where's Adam anyway?"

"On the other side of the bar tonight. Or he should be, anyway. I don't think he's arrived yet." Cooper gave me one last smile, then turned back to the group of guys clustered around his side of the bar.

I focused on mine and for once things went okay. No one wanted some fancy drink that wasn't on the main menu, so that was good.

"We're out of Captain Morgan!" Cooper shouted an hour later. "Could you run out and get a new bottle? No, make that more than one. Best to have some reserve."

"Yeah, sure." I switched places with another bartender who'd been in the back washing dishes, grabbed the key to the storage room, and got three bottles. I grabbed one Vodka too, because the one I'd used earlier didn't have much left in it and I wasn't sure if we had one extra or not.

I hurried back behind the bar. I changed out the top of one of the Captain Morgan bottles, put it on the shelf, then stacked the rest of them under the bar, out of sight from the customers.

"I'll be on washing up duty for a while, okay?" I

told Cooper, who was the one in charge tonight when Adam wasn't here.

He gave me the thumbs up, so I escaped all the noise and the bustle of the club to the dishwasher and the dirty glasses. The next tray was only started though, so I had to go back out and gather up more dirty glasses.

Oh well. It's better than being behind the bar.

I hadn't seen anything more of Wynn, or Chad for that matter. They'd stayed cooped up in his office and a small part of me wondered what they were doing in there. Wynn had said they'd used to sleep together before... but no. Wynn wasn't the kind of guy to sleep around and hadn't he said that Chad had two lovers? Surely he must already be sexually satisfied. And Wynn had just fucked *me*, so he was too.

"Kaz!"

A hand shot out from nowhere and locked around my wrist, squeezing hard. For a minute there I thought it was Wynn—but then I realised the person had used my nickname, not my real name, and my blood froze. I turned slowly and came face to face with Alistair.

Al didn't look happy. His face was all pinched, mouth pressed into a line, eyebrows drawn together in a glare. "Come with me."

I dropped the glasses I'd been holding in my other hand as he dragged me with him towards the employees-only area—and the back door. "Al, no—" If only I could get my hand out of his grip, I could make a run for it to Wynn's office... but I was too weak. The grip he had on me would bruise and it hurt and I didn't stand a chance.

The back door loomed in front of us. He slammed it open, then shoved me through and up against the alley wall before he slammed it closed again.

"Three days," he said, voice low, dangerously so, as he turned slowly to face me. "I've been waiting three days to hear from you. And nothing."

"I moved out. I left a note." I cowered against the wall. If I tried to run for the street, he'd only have more of an excuse to hurt me. "That should've been enough."

He stalked towards me and I reared back as far as I could, but the wall didn't give. "You can't just leave a note. You can't just grab all your stuff when I'm not home and decide you want to move out. That's our place."

"It's your place. It's your name on the lease." My name wasn't anywhere. Not even on the mailbox. For all intents and purposes, no one even knew I lived there if I didn't personally tell them.

He slammed a palm against the wall right next to my head. I flinched, but there was nowhere to go, so I had to stand my ground. "Weren't you going to tell me face to face? What? Are you too much a coward to say it out loud? So you leave a note?"

I *was* a coward, but who wouldn't be when faced with him? If he didn't understand why I'd chosen to leave a note instead of facing him...

"Kaz." Now his other palm slammed against the wall, on the other side of my head. He loomed over me, trapping me there in the alley, against his body. I had nowhere to go, no one to turn to because Wynn was in his office and he had no idea I wasn't behind the bar any more. "You don't understand how difficult it is for me—"

"Difficult?" I choked out. "How difficult it is for *you*? What about *me*?"

"It's not about you," he snapped. "You have no idea what it's like to be me. What I struggle with."

"Can't you struggle on your own instead of dragging me into it?" My bottom lip trembled and I was *this* close to crying. That I could still stand there and have a conversation with him was a miracle in itself. All I wanted was to curl into a ball and hope he'd be satisfied with one hit or one kick and then leave me to it. "I'm not your punching bag. I never volunteered to be that."

He gritted his teeth. "If you could just act fucking normal—"

"Normal!" That came out almost like a shriek. It

would've horrified me if I wasn't already so damn scared. "I *am* normal. I'm a human being, I've got feelings and wants and needs. Just because I don't fit into your perfectly macho, 'straight' world doesn't make me *abnormal*."

"You're such a fucking girl," he snarled. "Just look at you. You're *this close* to crying."

So he could see that, huh? I didn't think he ever saw anything but himself. "There's nothing wrong with showing emotions," I whispered. "Just because I'm a little more emotional than most people doesn't make it right what you—" I gasped as his palm slapped my cheek.

"Shut up, Kaz. Don't you dare start crying on me."

I covered my cheek with my hand, staring off to the side at the ground. "What do you want with me?"

"Move back in."

"No." My voice shook, but it held. It held enough for him to hear it, for it to hold some sort of conviction behind it. "I won't."

"Kaz…" His voice had a warning tone to it now. "I'm struggling here. You know that. You know my parents won't like it if I'm gay."

"That doesn't make it right, what you're doing." My cheek throbbed, but at least it had only been a slap of his palm and not a hit of his fist. "I shouldn't be afraid of you."

"Afraid of me?" That seemed to surprise him some-how. "Kaz, we're a couple, you and I."

"Not any more," I whispered, contemplating whether to duck under his arm and make a run for it. But no, he'd catch me and then he likely would use his fist. "I'm done."

"I'm not done!" He hit the wall several times in anger and I cowered, the tears overflowing. "Don't fucking cry! You always do that!"

"I'm sorry!" I didn't mean to, but he was scaring me and I knew what he was capable of and I was all alone... I wanted Wynn. Wynn would help me, if only he knew I needed it. My new phone was in my locker and I had nothing on me that would be of any help.

"I can't be openly gay, you get that?" He leaned close, face hovering close to mine. "Once I finish my engineering degree, I'm gonna get a good job. I can't let being gay stand in the way of that. People discriminate against gay people still, you know."

"Not everyone does," I mumbled.

"No, maybe not, but some do." He stared hard at me. "And you're not exactly subtle are you?"

"Then just let me go," I begged. "I won't be a bother to you. I'll stay away."

"But I don't want you to!" He grabbed the front of my shirt now, shook me twice, and then pulled me in close. I braced my hands on his chest for balance—but he seemed to take it as something else as his face came closer.

"No, don't!" I looked away. *Don't kiss me!* "I'm with someone else now."

He stilled. Dangerously so. "What?"

"You're the one who i-insisted on an o-open r-relationship." I didn't like the way his grip on my shirt tightened, the way his body froze up. "It goes both ways. When you were out sleeping with other p-people, so was I. And I f-found someone I like better th-than y-y-you." It wasn't technically the truth, because I hadn't been out shagging people; it was only Wynn.

He shoved me back and my head hit the brick wall hard. I managed to stay on my feet simply by clinging to the wall.

"You cheated on me?" he snarled.

"It wasn't cheating," I forced out through the stabbing pain in my head. "If it was, then you were cheating too every time you went straight." I had no idea if he'd slept with other guys or not, but I knew for a fact there'd been many girls.

His fists clenched and unclenched, his body rigid. "It's not the same."

"It so is!" I shouted, tired and in pain and resigned. "It is the same. Sex is sex no matter what, and if you want to be with someone you don't go and dip your dick in any other hole that feels good—or that makes you feel *straight*!" Why he couldn't just admit to being bisexual was beyond me—it always about him not wanting to be gay, but the fact he could be with girls... didn't that automatically make him bisexual? If he was actually gay, could he keep having sex with the wrong gender?

I sure couldn't get it up for females—their parts did nothing for me. If he liked both, then good for him, but he could admit it and stick to it, and figure out if he wanted a relationship or if he wanted to sleep around.

"You can't have it both ways, Al. Either you want to be with someone, and *only* them, or you want to shag around. It's one or the other; you can't have both." Not that I would take him back even if he swore and begged, but maybe the next poor person who got involved with him wouldn't have to suffer the way I had.

"You know *nothing*!" he yelled and the fist came flying too quickly for me to duck.

I fell, bracing my fall with my hands, but they still scraped against the uneven ground. I spat blood and I wasn't sure if it was my lip that was split or if I'd bitten myself. All I knew was I tasted blood and it didn't taste good.

He stood over me, breathing heavily. "You can't

leave me, Kaz," he said then, and his voice was begging me. "You can't leave me."

"I already have." My knees hurt too. The back door was a way off. Could I crawl over there? Would he grab me again if I tried? "I already have, Al. *Please*. Just leave me alone." My tears mixed with the blood and my body was wracked by deep sobs. "Please just leave me alone."

"Kaz…" He took a step towards me, but stopped when the back door was slammed open.

"Kasey?"

The familiar voice washed over me and now I sobbed from relief. *Wynn's here, he's not going to let Al hurt you anymore.* "Wynn!"

He stepped out, took one look at me on the ground, then he lifted his dark gaze to Alistair, who stood frozen.

"Wynn," I sobbed. *Help me*, was what I wanted to add to it, but the words wouldn't come. The sobs overtook me to the point I couldn't speak and it took all I had just to breathe through them.

But Wynn seemed to understand. He walked towards me… and then flew past—and there was a crunch as his fist connected to Al's face.

CHAPTER 13

*T*pushed up on my knees as Al stumbled back. Wynn packed a good punch, and now he aimed a second one at Alistair's face. Al fell after that one, crashing to the ground with a pained groan. He didn't get much reprieve though before Wynn was on him—and he pounded his fist into Al's face again and again and—

"Wynn!" Chad was there all of a sudden, grabbing hold of Wynn's shoulders and trying to physically force him away from Alistair.

My first thought was *just let him be, let him finish him*. Alistair deserved what Wynn gave him; a taste of his own damn medicine.

"Wynn, for fuck's sake!" Chad wasn't quite as big

as Wynn, but he was pretty fit too, and he managed to force Wynn back. "You want to go back to prison?" he shouted. "Or you want to help your boyfriend?"

That last one did it. Wynn stopped fighting Chad to get to Al… and he slowly turned around to look at me.

I stared back, tears still streaming down my face, blood still trickling from my lips. "Wynn," I choked out and then he was there, strong arms enveloping me in a gentle embrace.

"What'd he do?" he whispered against my ear. "What'd he do to you, Kasey?"

I clung to him, his shoulder, his neck, anywhere I could get a good grip on, and just *cried*. Cried at being cornered by Al, for being so afraid, for the pain he'd caused me, and cried in relief because Wynn was finally here and he wouldn't let anyone hurt me anymore.

"Kasey." My name came out on a sigh and he held me closer, tighter. "I've got you."

Al was still on the ground, but he was moving and groaning. Chad stood above him, grimacing slightly before glancing at Wynn and me. I must look horrible, so I buried my face in Wynn's neck.

"Come on, Kasey, we've got to go back inside."

I nodded and let him help me up on my feet. I didn't want to stay in the alley any more, not as long as

Al was still there. Still on the ground, but now on hands and knees, refusing to look at any of us.

Wynn wrapped a strong arm around my shoulders and led me inside and straight into his office.

Chad followed behind us. "Want me to bugger off?" he asked.

After pushing me down on the desk chair, Wynn straightened and ran a hand over his face. "He's not going back to work, so we're short-staffed out there. On a bloody *Saturday*."

I'd made a mess out of everything again. "I'm sorry." I bowed my head in shame.

"Hey." He ran a hand through my hair. "It's not your fault this happened."

I got a good look at the hand hanging loosely by his side and the knuckles... they were red and raw.

"I can watch your boytoy if you have to work," Chad shot in, grinning cheekily. Wynn stared him down, but Chad didn't seem to notice—or care. "I'd offer to bartend so you could stay with him, but we both know I don't know shit about mixing drinks. I'd probably just drink all the alcohol."

Wynn sighed heavily. The hand that had been in my hair now dragged over his face—and the knuckles on that one were sore too. Then he crouched down in front of me, putting both hands on my knees. "Do you want to go home? I can't leave them understaffed on a Saturday, so I've got to stay. For a few more hours at least. Chad can follow you home and look at your lip and I'll be there soon."

I softly put my palms on top of his hands, not daring to put any pressure on them with how raw they were after knocking Al around. "I hate that I keep making so much trouble for you," I whispered. "You had to take over for me on Tuesday too."

"Like I said, it's not your fault." He squeezed my knees. "Go home with Chad. You'll be safe there. And that arsehole is banned from my club as of now. He's not getting in here ever again."

I drew in a shaky breath. That was good to hear, at least. I nodded. "Okay, I'll go home."

He leant close, kissing my forehead, then drew me into another hug. "Give me a few hours, till the rush lets up. Cooper can take over from there."

I ran my hand over my mouth as I stood up, feeling how my lower lip had swollen on one side and some coagulated blood stuck to my skin. I still had a metallic taste in my mouth too, so I probably *had* bitten myself when Al hit me.

"Look after him," Wynn said to Chad, voice low and deep and threatening.

"I'll guard him with my life." Chad mock-saluted, then snorted. "Chill out, man, it'll be fine."

Wynn stopped me again as we exited his office, drawing me in close to kiss my temple. "Don't feel bad."

That was easier said than done.

After getting my phone and jacket from my locker, Chad and I exited the club from the main door. I couldn't stomach going through the back, especially as I didn't know if Alistair was still there or not.

"Is Wynn going to get in trouble?" I asked then, thinking back to how viciously he'd hit Al and how Al's face had looked a lot worse than mine.

He blew out an annoyed breath. "I doubt it. If that fucker dares to press charges, he was hitting you first, so Wynn would counter-sue his arse so bad he won't be able to walk."

The mental image that brought up startled me into a laugh.

He smiled too. "So how'd Wynn bank a sweetheart like you, huh? He's not the type to go on the pull and you're *nothing* alike Madison."

Madison… I knew I shouldn't, but… "You knew him? Madison?" When Chad only nodded, I dared ask some more. "What was he like?"

That made him grimace and for a second I thought I'd crossed a line. "Madison… he was a *freak*. Mind you, he was nice and all, but… he was so fucking *weird*. Obsessed with death, for one; not that I think he revealed much of that to Wynn, but he said some weird-arsed shit to me at the end there." His expression turned thoughtful. "He never minded that Wynn slept with me either, which is extremely weird, right? That you'd let your boyfriend shag someone else."

He blinked, seemed to realise who he was talking too, and then stepped closer. "Not that Wynn's the cheating type, mind. He isn't. At *all*. He's so loyal. But Madison was always weird about shit, like living and sex and *breathing*. And I know he must've had some horrible trauma in his life to turn out like he did, but... he wasn't ever up for much. Like intimacy or sex or any of that. And us normal people need some of that once in a while, right? And then I got with my guys and Madison was dead... and Wynn just kept existing, but he never went out looking for other people. I thought maybe he didn't need it anyway—maybe he only shagged me because I was manic and hypersexual and probably didn't give him much choice in the matter... but then I walked in on you two today." And that wicked grin was back.

I flushed at the reminder of just what he'd seen us do earlier.

"That was hot, by the way." He bumped my shoulder gently with his. "Wynn might have been facing the door, but he was too caught up in you to even notice me. And *that* sure doesn't happen often. Wynn's got eyes like a hawk—he notices *everything*."

That was... both flattering and embarrassing, as it made me blush even *more*. But it also made me smile. I tried to restrain it, but gave up and instead bowed my head.

"You really like him, huh?" He stretched his arms up, hooking his hands behind his neck, and stared up at the dark sky. "That's good. Wynn deserves some happiness in his life. He hasn't had much of it. And he seemed pretty happy with you."

I sure hoped he seemed happy. Besides the whole drama Al had instigated anyway. "It hasn't even been a week though," I murmured. I didn't know if Chad already knew or not, what Wynn had shared when they'd been cooped up in his office.

"Love at first sight?" He laughed. "Now that's rare."

"That doesn't happen," I argued meekly. "That's a cliché that only happens in romance novels and romantic films and love songs."

"Hey, don't diss the love at first sight trope." He just wouldn't stop grinning. "It does happen to some people. Some people even make it work."

I raised my eyebrows inquiringly. "Do you know of anyone?"

"Uhh..." He scratched the back of his neck. "Your

brother was pretty quick to fall into a relationship, as far as I've been told."

That surprised me as I hadn't realised he knew Kian was my brother. Had he recognised me all this time? I couldn't remember ever having met Chad before, though, come to think of it.

His ever-present grin was back. "Don't worry. Kian showed me a picture of you once when we were at the pub. You were in college. Had pink hair. I guess that's why I remember the face so well too."

Heh, my pink hair phase. I kind of missed it. Not that I wanted to go back to it—I was a bit too old for pink hair now.

We were at Wynn's building now, and... "Wynn forgot to give me his key." *Shit.*

"Not to worry." He brandished his own set of keys. "I've got one."

I blinked. "You've got a key to Wynn's flat?"

"Sure do." He grinned cheekily as he let us in. "I'm not allowed to use it though unless in an emergency. But this one counts, right?"

Emergency? What kind of emergency would that be? Had he used it *before*?

I trudged after him into Wynn's flat, toeing off my shoes in the hall. Chad disappeared into the bathroom and came back with cotton and antiseptic. We sat down and faced each other on the sofa, and I was quiet as I let him wash off the blood and clean my split lip. There wasn't much to do with the bite on the inside of my cheek, but at least my lip got a thorough clean. It was still swollen, but there wasn't much to do about that either.

Chad cleaned up after us. He clearly knew how anal Wynn was about cleaning too, because he only waggled his eyebrows teasingly as he left to deposit the used pads in the rubbish.

"What do you like to do to relax?" he asked once he came out of the bathroom. "And don't say sex."

"I wasn't going to," I murmured, flushing bright red again. "Um, I like to watch movies. Re-watch movies, anyway, that's always a good way to unwind."

He flung himself on the sofa. "All right. I can do a movie. Whatever you want."

I knew what I wanted and I walked over to where all my DVDs were stores. I was in pain and the encounter with Al had really shaken me, and Wynn wasn't here right now… so this called for Disney.

"What are we watching?" Chad asked, leaning over to get the remote so he could turn the TV on.

"Tangled." I hoped he wouldn't mind.

He seemed blank however. "Never heard of it."

Yeah, I reckon he wouldn't have. He was a grown man, shacked up with two other men, and so wasn't likely to be sitting around watching Disney's animated movies.

But I loved them and they cheered me up, much more than most of my anime, though watching those always left me in a good mood too. As did dance movies, but no, this kind of shitty night was definitely a Disney night.

CHAPTER 14

"*H*ey, Wynn?"

"Hmm?"

I lay halfway on top of him, head resting on his chest, arm over his waist, one leg tangled with his. Anime played on the telly and it was right in the middle of a fight scene, but it couldn't quite hold my attention. I'd seen it before, anyway.

Wynn, on the other hand, who'd said he'd watch it with me, was now reading a book. The same one I'd seen him reading yesterday—the gay smut novel. As long as I could use him for a pillow I didn't mind though. My taste in movies and series weren't for everyone—though Chad had seemed quite interested in Tangled last night.

"Chad said something last night…"

He sighed deeply, as if to say *oh boy, here it comes*. "What?"

"Nothing bad," I hurried to assure him so he wouldn't think the worst. "It's just, he said he wasn't allowed to use the key to your flat unless in case of emergency. And I just wondered… like, what kind of emergency would that be? Has he had to use it before?"

A beat of silence… then Wynn snapped his book shut and put it on the table. I tilted my head back to look up at him, curious and, if I was honest, slightly worried.

He stared straight ahead, not at the TV, but at the bare wall next to it. His brows were drawn together somewhat. "I get depressed," he murmured. "Or I used to. I manage it with medication and for the most part it works."

"But not always?"

"No." He sighed heavily. "Sometimes it gets really bad. It hasn't ever been as bad as it was after Madison died though. That landed me in the hospital for an overdose and then I was sectioned for a while. But… yeah. It can get pretty bad. To the point I can't get out of bed."

I'd had a fairly carefree childhood. Mum and Dad

had always been healthy, and we'd never had any issues with mental illnesses. Kian was healthy too, though he'd had a worse childhood than I'd had with his neglectful mum. But one of Kian's closest friends had it pretty bad—and Chad too, obviously, from what he'd revealed to me last night almost matter-of-factly.

"It happens once or twice a year, usually," he continued quietly. "It's turned into a pattern, really. Sometime during spring and then autumn."

Well, it was winter now, and he'd clearly got over it. *Not until spring then*. If the pattern continued. "What're you doing for Christmas?" I asked without actually meaning to. It was three weeks away, after all.

"What I always do. Stay here. Work. There's always paperwork to do when the club's closed."

That didn't sound like a particularly nice Christmas. "Don't you have family?"

"None that matters." And now his tone was final, as if this wasn't a subject he wanted to get into any further.

I took the hint and dropped it. *Must be bad then if he doesn't even see his family at Christmas*. "Maybe you could come home with me? Mum and Dad live outside of London and I always spend Christmas with them. Kian and Silver do too, except that one year they went home to Silver's parents but that didn't go so well, so now they always spend Christmas with us." That came out a bit more long-winded than necessary, but I was nervous he'd shoot me down immediately.

"You're asking me home to meet the family? It hasn't even been a week since we met." He chuckled.

"Yeah, well… by the time Christmas rolls around it'll have been a month." More than enough time to meet my parents, right? Al had never met them. I'd never been allowed to tell them about him.

He draped his arms over my shoulders. "I'm not very good with people."

"It's just my parents." I rubbed my nose against his chest.

"That's even worse, isn't it?" He sighed again. "I don't know, Kasey. People don't like me. Parents least of all."

"Have you been around many parents?" I asked drily, because really… how could he claim that? As far as I'd understood, and what he'd told me, he'd only had the one serious boyfriend.

"I'm just not a people person." He dragged a hand through his hair.

I stroked a hand over his chest. "Just think about it, okay? It's still a way off." I hoped he'd come. I didn't want him to stay alone over Christmas. And I did want my parents to meet him. My first *real* boyfriend, because that's what he was. Al hadn't ever been real, had he, because he'd been so deep in denial about everything… But Wynn didn't mind us being open about this. And I *liked* that, because I wanted to be open. I wanted to be able to mention my boyfriend, or stand close to him in public, or hold his hand, or even kiss him even if there were people around.

"I'm not making any promises," he said, "but yeah, I'll think about it."

"Great!" I didn't need anything more than that. We had three weeks to go—I'd work on him, wear him down. I tilted my head up for a kiss, but when he obliged me I was painfully reminded why I'd avoided kissing since last night. "Ow. Dammit."

"All right?" Wynn turned all worried, thumb stroking my cheek.

"Yeah, just this damn lip… And it hurts on the inside of my cheek too because I bit myself when he hit me last night." That was probably when, anyway, last night was a bit of a blur to be honest. Maybe I was repressing it… but no, I did remember it, it just—I wanted to get it at a distance.

Wynn's hand cupped my neck. "If Chad hadn't pulled me off I don't think I would've stopped hitting him."

"When Chad pulled you off I wanted you to

continue hitting him," I admitted in a low voice. "But I'm glad you didn't. I don't want you to get in trouble." I remembered clearly Chad asking him if he wanted to end up prison again. I reckoned the whole prison thing was what he'd already told me about his boyfriend and the drugs and whatnot. I didn't want to stir into that though, so I didn't mention it.

His chest rumbled as he chuckled darkly. "What a pair we make, huh?"

I'd completely lost interest in the anime playing on the telly and now I peered up at him. Blowing him wasn't going to happen today with my swollen lip, but we could do loads of things without me offering a BJ. He could do it or he could fuck me or—

He grinned wryly. "I know that look." He moved, rolled us over so I was on my back and he stretched out over me. "What do you want?"

"I don't know. I'm trying to figure it out." I wanted it all. Both a blowjob and a fuck. When it came to fucking I wanted it all there too; slow and fast and hard. "Everything. All the things. Do whatever you want to me."

His grin turned decidedly wicked and then he buried his face in my neck, sucking the thin skin. I tilted my head away, giving him space. I also lifted one leg to rest over his hip and arse while I spread the other wider so our crotches rubbed together.

"Whatever I want?" He squeezed my dick through my pyjama trousers—I still hadn't got dressed properly, and as we planned on spending our whole day inside, I didn't plan on dressing properly until tomorrow anyway.

"Anything you want," I confirmed. "As long as it's not anything to do with my mouth." Damn Alistair and his fists. How long would it take for the swelling to go down? For the split to heal properly? Not to mention the bite inside my mouth… that was a little swollen now too and it really hurt if I so much as brushed my tongue over it. When could I kiss Wynn again? When could I suck his cock? Because I really, really wanted to do both of those things.

His hand, big and warm, slipped under my clothes and fisted my dick. I arched my hips up, or tried anyway, as he lay on top of me, keeping me firmly down against the soft sofa.

"Impatient?" he asked, lips brushing over my cheek, down to my ear, where he nibbled gently on my earlobe.

"Mmm," was all that came out of me as he squeezed my dick in a particular way just then, already wringing pre-come from me.

"Do you want to pause your cartoons?"

"*Anime*. Not cartoons," I argued.

"Same difference." He licked down my neck again,

then attached his mouth to thin skin, sucking and prob-ably making another hickey. I didn't mind. Hell, I *wanted* him to. "So?"

"It's not necessary. I've seen it before." I knew what happened. I'd seen it more than once, if I was going to be entirely honest.

"Then we can just turn the damn telly off. It's distracting." He did so and then dove right back to my neck.

I clutched at his shoulders, wishing I could drag him up into a deep kiss, but I knew that wouldn't be possible at all today. Or tomorrow. Or maybe not even the day after. *Dammit.*

He was still fisting my cock, stroking entirely too slow. "You can hurry up, you know," I pointed out in a dry, impatient tone. "In fact, please *do*."

His chest rumbled. "You're definitely impatient."

I was. So damn much. If only he knew just how much I wanted to get off right now—

The doorbell rang.

"The fuck?" This was not how it was supposed to go.

Wynn looked up with a slight frown. "Chad didn't say anything about stopping by today."

"Can we ignore it?" My dick was desperate to keep his hand exactly where it was.

The bell rang again.

"I guess not." He sighed and heaved himself off me. "Whoever it is can fuck off though."

I righted my clothes, but didn't move from my position. Best to lie there ready for when Wynn came back. I listened to him walk over the floor, then heard the door unlock and crack open. Then… nothing. Not a sound.

I rolled onto my side and pushed up on my elbow so I could look over at Wynn. The door was open and he was locked in a staring contest with whoever was on the other side. My stomach clenched. *I've got a bad feeling about this.* It better not be Al. If it was… well, I wouldn't stop Wynn if he decided to beat his face in again.

"Kasey." Wynn turned away from the door, dark gaze finding me. "It's for you." He waved at the door before walking off to the kitchen.

"What?" It couldn't be Al. Wynn wouldn't have left the door open if it was him. I jumped off the sofa to investigate. "Kian?"

He stood on the other side of the door, with Silver behind him. Kian glared, Silver looked like he'd rather be anywhere else. "You never said you lived with someone," Kian said, crossing his arms.

"Umm." No, I hadn't said that. Still… Did he remember the address when I'd only mumbled it to him once?

"So, funny story." Kian glanced back at Silver, who refused to look at him in turn. "We were having lunch at Harriet's, discussing whether to show up for a visit unannounced or not when we met Chad... and he tells us you live with Wynn."

"I was going to tell you," I mumbled. "Eventually."

Kian frowned even harder. "What happened to your lip?"

My hand shot up to it, accidentally jarring the swollen area, and I cursed inwardly as pain shot through me. "Umm..." *Shit*. I'd never wanted to tell Kian the truth about Alistair. He'd always liked Al a lot, even if our relationship had always been a secret. Not that he knew that was a stipulation set by Al, though, as I'd always told him I wanted to keep it on the down-low too. *There's just so many lies...*

I glanced over my shoulder. Wynn was still in the kitchen, back to me, but he'd put the kettle on. "Might as well invite them inside," he said.

I guess it's time. I stepped away, leaving the way inside clear for them. Kian all but marched in, but Silver was more hesitant. He met my gaze, smiled slightly, but his eyes zeroed in on my lip too and his expression turned more worried.

My dick had certainly deflated, so our interrupted moment was definitely ruined. No need to worry about unwanted boners, that was for sure. "Sit down." I motioned to the sofa.

Kian sat on one end, but he didn't seem happy about it. Silver plopped down next to him, still frowning, gaze locked on me. I perched on the edge of the other side, glancing at Wynn and wishing he'd join me.

And he did, with cups of tea. *Tea, dammit. So this isn't going to be over in a whiff.* One look at Kian told me he wasn't going to let it go either.

"Did he do that?" Kian asked, all but glaring at my lip, but his jab was obviously meant for Wynn, for whom he didn't spare a single glance.

"Umm." I swallowed, gaze flickering. "No."

"If you're lying to me, Kaz, I swear to God I'll—"

"This is the first time in a long time I'm *not* lying to you," I interrupted, the words falling out of me in a hurry.

Kian sat back a little in surprise, blinking.

I closed my eyes, sighed, then opened them again and inched a little closer to Wynn. He looked at me, seemingly the calmest one here at the moment.

Time to tell my brother the truth, then. Maybe it would be for the best. *Time to stop lying to him. To them.* They were my family after all. Surely they would believe me? *Of course they will,* a voice chastised me, but it was still hard to be so sure when Al had told me over and over again that no one would believe me if I ever spoke the truth of our relationship or our living situation or his behaviour towards me.

"Who did it then?" Kian asked, a little meeker than before, but still determined.

I drew in a shaky breath. *Here goes then.*

CHAPTER 15

"*A*listair did it." I folded my hands and rested them in my lap, foot jiggling nervously, and teeth nibbling on my lower lip. "It's not the first time either."

Silver's expression hardened. Kian's turned slack in surprise. "Alistair?"

I nodded quickly.

"But…" This had taken Kian completely by surprise. "But—why?"

Now I shrugged. "I don't know. He just… liked slapping me around. He did it often enough."

Kian had a hard time wrapping his head around this, I could tell. Silver was more difficult to read. "But he's always so *nice*."

"Of course he is around other people." A chuckle

left me, but it wasn't a happy one—more bitter, if anything. "No one can know he likes to fuck guys and then abuse them afterwards, because he can't deal with his own sexuality."

Silver bent forward a little while Kian wrapped his head around what I was saying. "How long has this been going on?"

I didn't dare look at either of them so I kept my head bowed. "Since I met him, really. He… didn't want to come out. To anyone, ever. And I went with it because I liked him so much. It wasn't until I moved in with him I realised how horrible he really was."

Wynn sat motionless next to me. No one had touched the tea. I didn't think I could drink anything with the way my stomach was clenching tight in anxiety.

"I've wanted to move out for a long time, but I couldn't move back to Mum and Dad with my job here and all. And you guys… you don't really have the space." It was all said to the floor. "Then I met Wynn… and he's great. He helped me. Helped me move out, helped me last night when Al had dragged me outside to try to—I don't know, get me back, I guess? But he didn't like what I had to say so he hit me, and then Wynn was there and he saved me and just—" God, I was rambling.

"He's been nothing but nice to me. He likes me

exactly how I am and he doesn't mind that people know about us. He's not going to try and change me and he's not going to insist on separate bedrooms and secrets and never telling anyone about our real relationship. He won't cheat on me." Hopefully, anyway. But even Chad had said Wynn was loyal and as his best friend he should know better than anyone what Wynn was like. I'd only known him a week, so I couldn't say yet, but the way he'd treated me so far… it was better than anyone had ever treated me.

"Kaz…" Kian was up off the sofa and plastered against my side in an instant, hugging me so close he nearly obstructed my airways. "I never—shit, I don't know—I never *saw* it."

I didn't hold a grudge against him. Of course not. I knew Al was manipulative. He was all charming in public. The kind of person every mother would be happy for her child to date. It was only in private he changed… "It's not your fault." I glanced at Silver and he stared back.

"I kinda suspected," he said, surprising both me and Kian.

"What? You did? Since when?" Kian demanded, but he didn't release his hold on me. "You never said…"

"I didn't *know*." He bent forward, arms dangling between his knees. "I just thought you changed a lot all of a sudden. Mathilda, who was your best friend for a long time... I mean, you pretty much stopped being her friend. And this is the girl who you worried so much about after her dad died and she went off the deep end for a bit. It was *weird*. I just couldn't pinpoint why. I couldn't tell it was Alistair. He was her friend too, right?"

Silver was the more perspective one of them. Kian was sweet and caring, but he could be a bit oblivious at times. He had such a good life that as long as something wasn't physically wrong with someone else, he had a hard time catching on sometimes. "He is. She doesn't know... and now she's in France and I haven't talked to her in months. Even if I did talk to her I have no idea what I'd say."

"The truth?" Kian suggested.

"I don't want to ruin her friendship with Alistair. No matter what he was to me, he's a good friend to other people." To Mathilda and Nick, at least, they'd been a trio ever since they started A-levels. I hadn't been a part of it, but Mathilda and I had bonded through dance and I'd fancied Alistair *so much* and Nick had ended up becoming Adam's boyfriend. Even back then Adam had been a good friend of mine; a result of both our older brothers being close friends, we'd kind of been forced together in the beginning and then hit it off.

Kian tilted his head against mine. "I can't believe he'd be so cruel to you. You're the sweetest guy I know."

"He's got issues," I murmured. I didn't hate Alistair… not really. I pitied him, was more like it. I'd always known I was gay and I'd never had any problem with it. But then my parents had always been open and honest and supportive. I'd never been afraid they wouldn't accept me for exactly who I was.

"That doesn't excuse it." Kian finally relented his tight grip around me, green eyes glancing briefly at Wynn, who sat leant back next to me, elbow on the arm of the sofa, chin in palm. "How long have you two—? Ever since you started working at the club?"

"Oh, no," I hurried to say, because really… did he think I'd been living with Al and been with Wynn for two whole *months* before things changed? "Only a week, really. It's not that long, I know, but…" I trailed of, not sure what I'd been about to say.

Kian hitched his eyebrows. "A week? And you're living together?"

"Yeah, well…" I glanced at Wynn but for once he was no help, sitting there all quiet like a clam. Then again, this was my brother, his boyfriend; they were my family and Wynn had clearly told me he wasn't good with people. "You're one to talk." I jumped on the defensive. "You practically moved in with Silver after you shagged him too."

"I didn't *officially* move in. I still lived with Chloe for *months*," he pointed out.

"Still, you spent almost every night with him." I sighed. "We're doing okay so far. I mean, as long as we're both fine with the situation there's nothing wrong with it right?" And yes, maybe it was weird to live together when it'd only been a week, but did it matter? We were fine. We were getting to know each other. And if we worked out... we'd continue living together anyway. If we didn't... well, then I'd have to figure something else out. "You can't know how things will turn out unless you try. And you two've been doing wonderfully for years now."

I'd always been jealous of what they'd had. I'd fancied Silver when Kian had first brought him around —fancied him *a lot*—but it'd been obvious he and Kian were made for each other. Silver was calm where Kian could be excitable. He was tall and muscular and tattooed, where Kian was small and slim and pale. They were opposites, yet they fit so nicely together.

Wynn and I... we were opposites too. I could only dream of the kind of relationship Kian and Silver had —but maybe that dream wasn't so far off now? Maybe I could have that too... That was all I'd ever wanted, after all. Even botching my audition wasn't so bad if I could only have someone who liked me as much as I liked them, who didn't treat me horribly, and like I was a dirty little secret.

"Wynn treats me well," I said then, voice clear and *sure*. "He would never hurt me like Al's done. He hurt Al last night—but he'd never raise his fist to me." Wynn's hands were always so gentle. Speaking of… I reached out and grabbed his hand, squeezing tightly, and giving him a small smile when he glanced at me. "I like what we have so far." I wasn't sure if I was speaking to him now or my brother. I was still looking at Wynn anyway, so it was probably mostly meant for him—and if it gave Kian some peace of mind in the process too, then that was good. "I want to see how we do from here. I think… we'll be good together."

I had so much love to give. And I didn't think he'd ever received any. Maybe from his dead boyfriend, but… from what Chad had said about him, it probably hadn't been the healthiest of relationships. I might've been damaged by Alistair… but because of that, I definitely knew what *not* to do in a relationship. And I had good role models in my brother and his boyfriend; they'd started as a one-off and had been together for years. There was nothing against Wynn and I ending up like that too. We *could*. No one knew, because no one could tell what the future held.

And wasn't that a little nice? That there was an

endless stretch of time ahead of us, where no one could tell what would happen, and only we ourselves could work for the best outcome?

"Well, you sure look happier now," Silver pointed out, leaning back with a small smile. "I don't think I've ever seen you smile as much before."

I scratched the back of my neck awkwardly.

Kian smirked. "Well, granted, when he was younger he was too busy blushing over you, babe, to ever be able to show his face much."

"Now, come on—" Did he have to bring *that* up? I knew I'd been pretty obvious, but hell. Silver was sitting right *there*. Not to mention Wynn—he didn't need to know I'd fancied my brother's boyfriend back when I was a teenager.

Wynn squeezed my hand, bringing my attention to him. I smiled, albeit it in embarrassment. That wry grin of his was in place.

Kian bumped me gently. "You were so adorable back then."

"Was not," I mumbled.

"You were. Fancying Silver so much…" He bumped me lightly again. "And then, well, then I guess Al happened and you didn't—I don't know. I never noticed it. Maybe because we didn't grow up together so I didn't know you all that well…"

That was true. Kian had only been in our lives a few months by the time he'd met Silver, after all.

"But you clearly had some suspicions." He cast a narrowed look at Silver.

Silver shrugged. "I knew him even less than you. For the first couple of years he hardly ever spoke in my presence, after all." I blushed at that, because yeah, it was totally true. "And then when he told us about Alistair and it was all such a secret… Hell, I don't know. It's weird, is all. Even Damian is more open about his emotions than you two were about your relationship, and Damian's so closed-off at times he might as well be a rock."

I snorted, thinking about his best friend.

Kian clapped his hands together, turning to me again. "How about dinner tomorrow? In a *restaurant*? Because we can do that now, right?"

I drew back in surprise. Kian had asked me before if Al and I wanted to go out for dinner, but Al had always shut that down. He was more than happy to go over to their place for dinner—to charm them—but out in public with two femme gay guys? No way.

"Yeah, sure," Wynn said, speaking for the first time since Kian and Silver had entered his flat. "Jeremy's new restaurant is quite good."

"Jeremy?" I asked faintly, surprised he'd said yes and yet giddy with the simple thought that he didn't mind being out in public with me. He'd even go out with my brother and his boyfriend! He, who only a little while ago, had kept insisting he wasn't a people person.

"One of Chad's guys," he explained. "He's a chef."

"Oh, right." I hadn't known that, but then I didn't know Chad. He hadn't said much about his two boyfriends the night before. Mostly, we'd quietly watched the movie and then Wynn had been home, so it had been time for Chad to leave.

"I didn't know he'd switched jobs," Kian said, beaming. "But sure, we can go there. Just give us the details and we'll sort out a time, and meet up tomorrow, okay?"

My heart beat in my chest.

I had a new boyfriend and Kian didn't seem to dislike him as much as I'd thought he did. Maybe now he'd actually met Wynn—with me—his perception of him had changed. I sure hoped so. They were all even willing to go to dinner. I gripped the front of my jumper, over my heart. I could feel it beat and I bowed my head as a smile slowly stretched my lips.

Is this happiness?

Then it's nothing like anything I've ever felt before.

If it was… it was wonderful. A week wasn't a long time, but it was long enough to change my life around completely.

CHAPTER 16

"*I*'m getting a strong sense of déjà vu again."

I sniffled and wiped at my eyes, turning my head slightly to look at Wynn, who leant against the bedroom doorway. "I'm sorry, it's just—" I wiped some more on my face, trying to be rid of the damn tears. "I get so emotional. I'm just happy is all."

"Yeah?" He came into the room, advancing on me slowly. "That sure is a difference to the night we met."

I laughed through my tears. "It is, isn't it?"

His big hand settled on the top of my head, ruffling my hair.

"Mum always says I'm so sensitive. I cry easily. Always have. I'm sorry." It was a weakness, but I couldn't help it. When the tears pressed, I couldn't hold them back.

"Don't apologise." He crouched down in front of me, hand slipping from my head to rest on my knee. "There's nothing wrong with crying. Some people cry a lot, some don't cry at all. We're all different."

"You're probably in the *doesn't cry at all* category," I commented, chuckling a little.

"Mostly, yeah." He smiled slightly. "I've cried my share though." He put his other hand on my other knee. "Like when Madison died. After that wasn't a good time."

"What was he like?" I asked, remembering what Chad had said, but wanting to hear how Wynn had seen his previous boyfriend.

His lips flattened and he bowed his head so I couldn't see his expression. I regretted asking, thinking he wouldn't answer me, but then he started speaking. "He wasn't anything like you."

I started. What was that supposed to mean? Was it good? Bad? Or was it just an observation that didn't really mean anything?

"He was… distant, I guess. But…" He had a hard time finding the words. It was obvious he wasn't used to speaking about this. "He was a sweetheart, really. He just… His life was shit. His mum was a bitch. And because of his horrible childhood he had a lot of problems. He didn't even want to tell me most of what had happened to him during his childhood, so I don't know much of it." His grip around my knees tightened. "Mine was probably nothing compared to his though."

I leant forward a little so I could rest my cheek against the top of his head. *What was your childhood like then?* I wanted to ask, but I didn't want to push. The fact he was talking about Madison was a bit surprising on its own. We had time to talk about his childhood later—I didn't need to know now. Even if he never wanted to talk about it, that was fine. I knew him now. I liked the person he was now.

"I knew he had a bit of an interest, or obsession maybe, with death and dying. I just never thought—I never thought he'd do it. Back then it was really hard, especially considering I was thrown in jail and wasn't even allowed to go to his funeral. I tried to… well, I overdosed and ended up sectioned, so I guess that was rock bottom. Things were hard without him. I had no one anymore—Chad was busy dealing with his own illness and he had his guys. I'd only had Madison." He paused. "Nowadays though… I like to think he's better wherever he is now. That he's not struggling or suffering or worrying. That he's finally at peace."

I wrapped my arms around his neck. I hadn't lost anyone—except my grandparents on both Mum and

Dad's side, but I'd been young then—so I couldn't imagine what it would be like.

"And sometimes I think—" He drew in a shaky breath. "That perhaps he's better off dead. Like, when he was alive everything was so difficult for him. Life, being sociable, being with someone, not being with someone... everything was a struggle. And now nothing is, because he's at peace. I hope he is anyway. No, I *think* he is. He—yeah, he's good now. Living isn't for everyone and he's better off now."

I held him tight. I could tell from the way his voice had gone all hoarse and deeper that this was difficult to admit. "I like to think that everyone who dies is at peace. Maybe they're watching over us or maybe there's nothing at all after death, but whatever it is, it's peaceful."

He made a sound, something between a chuckle and a snort. He pulled away from me and finally lifted his head. His eyes were a little glassy, but other than that I saw no sign of tears. "Yeah. That's what I like to think too." He bowed his head again for a little while, gathering himself. When he looked back up, the glassiness was gone too and he grinned wryly. "So, dinner with your brother and his boyfriend tomorrow?"

"I hope you didn't feel pressured into saying yes to that," I said, anxiety flooding me. "We can cancel if you want."

"I wouldn't have said yes if I didn't want to." He straightened, patting my head, then looped his hand around my neck as he sat down next to me. *Right* next to me, so our thighs and sides pressed together. "Your brother loves you. He wants what's best for you. And frankly, so do I. I hope—well, yeah, that I can be that person."

A flush crept up my neck and bled into my cheeks. "You're already well on your way to being that, you know. No matter how sudden it is, it's true."

"It *has* only been a week," he mused, staring out at the room at large, one arm bracing him on the bed while the other was still around my neck. "But a relationship's got to start off somewhere, after all. There's got to be a certain amount of like and chemistry to make it work, and eventually…"

"Eventually?" I asked when he didn't continue.

He grimaced slightly. "Well, hopefully the like will bloom into love after a while, yeah?"

I smiled. "Yeah. I hope so. I like you a lot already."

"I like you a lot too." He drew me in close to press a chaste kiss to my temple. "Have for a while." And yes, that was true… he'd watched me before that night a week ago when we met. I tended to forget that, that he'd watched me long before I ever noticed him.

"You're the best thing that's happened to me," I murmured, curling in close to him.

He snorted. "Give it a while. I'm hardly that."

"You *are*," I pressed. "Even Kian and Silver noticed it." Speaking of… "They interrupted us. Maybe we should continue where we left off?"

"Yeah?" He moved close for a kiss—then froze.

"What?" I blinked.

"I keep forgetting about your lip."

"Oh." *Right*. My damn swollen, sore lip. "There are a lot of other places you can kiss though," I suggested.

Now he smirked. "Oh, I plan on kissing them, all right."

A gasp left me as he suddenly shoved me down on the bed, but when his warm, hard body covered mine and his lips attached to my neck, all I could do was sigh happily. "You're so good to me," I whispered.

"Shouldn't I be?" he asked drily.

I tried to suppress the wide smile, but failed majorly. "You better be. We're wearing too many clothes though. You should do something about that."

He stripped me slowly, taking his time kissing over the skin that was revealed. He spent extra time on my nipples once my jumper was off, sucking them into hard little nubs before he moved further down. His lips were warm and soft, such a contrast to the slight rasp of stubble. His tongue, when he licked my dick, was hot.

"I wish I could suck you too," I murmured, gazing down at him.

"Not with that lip you can't." His eyes, dark as ever, flicked up to stare at me. "But don't worry. I'll make you feel good. You just lie back and enjoy yourself."

I did. I closed my eyes and simply enjoyed. His hands on my skin, sliding the rest of my clothes off, his tongue, his lips, his mouth on me. All that existed in my tiny little world right then was him. His fingers, longer and thicker than mine, coated with lube and sliding into me. He fucked me gently with his fingers, crooking them a little in search of my prostate. When he found it my world narrowed even further.

When his cock slid into me, all I could do was cling to him. To the wide, strong shoulders that protected me, that I could lean on and cry on. He didn't judge me and I didn't annoy him and he wasn't embarrassed about being seen with me. He didn't care about any of that.

"Kasey…" He moved my legs so they rested on his shoulder, bending me in half. "Is this okay?"

"Y-yeah," I choked out, because *yes* it was! And he was hitting the right spot just perfectly.

"Good." He quickened his speed, thrusting his hips back and forth, driving his cock deep inside me, right up against my prostate.

I blinked my eyes open to watch him. His face was close to mine, face set in a sort of determined, intense expression, and sweat beaded on his forehead. He looked so fucking good. I grabbed his face, brought it even closer and kissed him. Only that wasn't a good idea at all—and I turned my head away with a hiss of pain.

He stopped thrusting, stayed buried inside me, and instead cupped my cheek. "You all right?"

"Ahh, yeah." I berated myself silently for trying to kiss him when I knew I had a swollen lip. Except I'd forgotten all about that in passion and now I suffered for it. "Sorry. I forgot."

He chuckled, leaning down to kiss my cheek, then the corner of my mouth—on the other side of where my lip was all sore and swollen. "Kissing won't be a thing for the next few days. Not for you at least."

"You feel free to kiss me wherever you want except there." I felt the skin around my lip. It was a little tender too. *Dammit.*

"Do you want to continue?"

What kind of question was that? "Do you want to stop?"

He chuckled. "No."

"Good. It's my lips that's busted, not anything else." Definitely not anything else. Though my dick had wilted a little after my dumb attempt at a kiss.

His hand wrapped around it, like he'd read my thoughts. "Stop trying to kiss me and we'll get this show back on the road." He grinned wickedly, moving his hips again in time with his fist stroking my cock.

Since he'd sat up now and there was no shoulder for me to hold on to, I let my arms flop to the bed. A soft moan left me and my eyes fluttered closed again as he quickened his thrusts.

"You look so sweet like this, Kasey," he said. "All flushed and spread open for me."

Him saying that only made me flush more. But his words also made me happy. He always praised me. Al had never done that. No one had ever done that before, not the guys I'd sucked off either. But Wynn... he always said nice things during sex. He was quite talkative, wasn't he?

"Do you like to take it from behind?"

He just wasn't going to let me lie still and enjoy this in quiet, was he? "Umm, yeah."

"Let's do that then." He pulled out, his dick still as hard as ever, the condom glistening with lube, the piercings trapped underneath it. He grabbed my hips and flipped me over before I could even think about moving. Getting an eyeful of his cock pretty much ensured I wouldn't be able to think, so... yeah. Good thing he took charge.

I got my knees under me and lifted my lower body off the bed.

"Fuck." He grabbed my arse, squeezing, spreading my cheeks. The head of his dick bumped against my opening, then slid in without any resistance.

A low, drawn-out moan escaped me and I buried my face in the sheets.

"You can make a noise," he said, leaning over me, hands running from my hips and up to brace against my shoulder-blades as he quickened his thrusts. "How many times do I have to tell you that? You don't have to be quiet with me. I want to hear you." He did a particularly hard, deep thrust, and I couldn't hold the groan in. "There you go."

"It's so good," I whispered, wanting him to know just how much I enjoyed this. Being loud in bed was embarrassing, but I could definitely *tell* him. Tell instead of show… *Hah. Shouldn't it be show instead of tell?* I'd work on it. If Wynn didn't think it was embarrassing, then it wasn't right?

He kept his thrusts up, hitting my prostate so good each time I felt like I might burst. And I did—I came without touching my dick and a few tears leaked out from the corner of my eyes. *Damn, even during sex I cry now.* But that was because it was so damn good. Because Wynn knew what he was doing, knew how to make my body react to every single thing he did. *He already knows me so well like this.*

His thrust grew a little erratic, his breath stuttering as he came too.

My knees gave out and he followed me down, body covering mine. He was heavy, but I didn't mind. It was nice to be so completely surrounded by him. It was so *safe*. Whenever he was around I didn't have to be afraid.

"I'll be right back." He brushed a kiss over the nape of my neck, then extracted himself from me. His dick, now flaccid, popped out of me and he pulled off the condom as he padded over the floor to the bathroom.

I hugged the pillow close, not caring right now that I lay in the middle of a wet spot. I'd have to get up eventually, and we'd have to change the sheets—or the duvet cover, anyway, but for now I was too content to bother with anything.

"Was it that good?" He laughed as he came into the bedroom again.

My gaze zeroed in on his dick and the piercings glinting in the light. It was... fascinating. I couldn't stop looking.

"Did I leave you speechless?" He bent over me, pressing a harder kiss to the nape of my neck.

"Umm." His dick was so close now. I grabbed it,

cupping it in my palm, rubbing my thumb over the piercings. "I just really like these."

He chuckled. "My piercings?"

"Mmm." I cupped his balls too. They were round, heavy.

"You've changed a lot in the past few days, you know."

"Hmm?" I finally tore my gaze away from his dick to look up into his eyes. "How so?"

"Well, for starters, you're not a bundle of anxiety anymore." He leaned down again, nose rubbing against the top of my head. "And that deer-caught-in-headlights-look… that's gone too." He climbed on the bed and stretched out next to me. I still fondled his dick, not letting it go, but I did arrange myself so I rested against him now instead of the pillow.

He wrapped an arm around my shoulders, holding me close. "It was all his fault, wasn't it?"

"Yeah." And it was true. Al had made me afraid of everything. Of people finding out, of people simply talking to me or being annoyed by me, like he always was. But Wynn… he made me feel safe and he never put me down. In fact, he'd helped me up, hadn't he? When I couldn't deal with the job, he'd taken me under his wing had properly taught me how to mix all kinds of drinks himself. No one else had ever done that. "This is better, right?"

His grip around my shoulders tightened. "Lots better."

And I smiled against his chest. I might've been slapped around and bruised by Alistair. Wynn and I might not love each other yet, but we liked each other a hell of a lot. We were compatible. And love always started with like, didn't it?

It was hard to say after only a week if we'd make it, but so far we were good. I was living with him already, we were good together, we got along, we had great sex... That was a good foundation to build on.

I knew I had my bad sides and he likely did as well, and we'd figure each other out eventually as we continued to live together... but that was what it was supposed to be like. We were supposed to experience both the good and the bad in each other, and then move on from there. Accept it, fight about it, whatever... I didn't think we wouldn't ever fight, because all couples did that from time to time. I didn't think we'd always be this content and calm, because that wasn't what life was like.

But we liked each other. We wanted to try and build from this. We wanted to be together. We wanted a relationship with each other. And yes, it had only been a week, but we'd already built a strong foundation. I wholeheartedly believed that.

A strong foundation was needed for when love

came along, for when life got hard again. With that strong foundation, it would be hard to knock it all down. Mutual like and respect... that was good. That was what had lacked previously. With Wynn, it didn't.

"I really like you," I whispered.

He grunted. "Good. Because I really like you too." And he kissed the top of my head, and I smiled, and for that moment everything was perfect.

Yeah, love can definitely be built on this.

ABOUT THE AUTHOR

TT lives in Norway and writes about gay men living in Norway. She also occasionally writes about gay men living in the UK, because she loves the UK. Norway might be too cold for her, but TT doesn't like the summer, so she's learned to adapt. TT is happiest in front of her computer, creating emotional stories about men loving other men.

www.ttkove.com
ttkove@gmail.com